I Carried You Home

I CARRIED YOU HOME

Alan Gibney

Patrick Crean Editions
An imprint of HarperCollins*PublishersLtd*

Published by Patrick Crean Editions, an imprint of HarperCollins Publishers Ltd

First edition

HarperCollins books may be purchased for educational, business,
or sales promotional use through our Special Markets Department.

HarperCollins Publishers Ltd
2 Bloor Street East, 20th Floor
Toronto, Ontario, Canada
M4W 1A8

www.harpercollins.ca

Library and Archives Canada Cataloguing in Publication
information is available upon request

ISBN 978-1-44344-453-8

Printed and bound in the United States of America
RRD 9 8 7 6 5 4 3 2 1

For Brendan

I Carried You Home

I.

THE POLICE SAID Will landed on the hood of the car, but I imagined it differently at the time. I imagined him flying over the hood and hitting the ground and everything going quiet and still, and it staying like that for a long moment, the snow falling gently on the wreck, and then the wind starting up again and her waking with the noise and pulling herself free and shouting into the trees, searching until she found him in the snow. She didn't think of dragging him to the car and leaving him on the seat and going for help. She wasn't capable of leaving him. She carried him on her back through the blizzard, up and down the steep hills, over the ice and snow. She kept forgetting what had happened. Why was she there? Why did her face hurt? A ditch. A tree. Keep moving. She was bent over, balancing him on her back, his arms over her shoulders. She shuffled forward, holding his wrists, his face against her neck. Her hands burned in the wind. How far was it? She drove it every day. It was at least a mile. Three long hills, a good mile. Will groaned and kicked his legs. Hold on, she shouted. He coughed against her neck. Something warm rolled down her back. We're almost there. Her teeth hurt, her neck hurt. She pulled down on his wrists to stop him struggling. Hold on.

I was doing homework in the living room, watching the snow swirling around the garden lights. I saw someone coming up the driveway, an old woman bent over carrying a bundle on her back, her long hair whipping in the wind. She looked up, and it was my mother, her face pale blue in the porch light. I ran outside in my T-shirt.

—What happened? What happened? I shouted over the wind.

—Who is it? Who am I carrying? she said. I saw Will's swollen face against her back.

—Will.

—Will? Open the door.

He groaned and struggled to get free.

—Open the door! For God's sake!

She climbed the porch stairs, crouching low, her legs shaking, and in the hallway, she knelt down and rolled Will onto the floor.

—Jesus. What happened? she said.

—You must have crashed.

—*No.* No. Will.

She ran her hands over his face. Blood was coming from his mouth.

—Do something, she said. Call someone. Hurry. Hurry. My boy. My lovely boy. Call someone.

I ran into the kitchen and phoned the ambulance service.

—There's been a crash. My mother and brother, they crashed. She carried him through the storm.

The woman told me to calm down and explain what had happened.

—I don't know. He's bleeding from his mouth. They crashed. My mom can't remember anything.

I gave our address and phone number. She said someone was on the way.

I phoned the Simses down the road and Mr. Sims answered.

—They had a crash, I said.

—What? What did you say?

—It's Ashe. Mom crashed her car. Will's hurt real bad. She carried him home on her back.

—At your house?

—Yes. Can you come? Please.

—We'll be there in two minutes. Hang on, son.

I went into the hallway.

—Did we crash? Did we? she asked.

—Yes.

She kept forgetting. I had to repeat it over and over.

—What's wrong with Will? He keeps falling asleep. Wake up!

—You're bleeding, I said.

She put her hand to her lips and looked at her fingers.

—My hand's frozen.

—You carried him home.

She looked at me. Her eyelids were red.

—The ambulance is coming, I said. I called the Simses. They'll be here in a minute.

—Ashe, I don't know what to do. I can't think straight. We

3

need to do something now, before it's too late. What's wrong with him? Why is he sleeping? Is that right?

—You crashed the car.

—He's all cut up, she said. Look at his scalp. He shouldn't sleep. Should he? I don't think so, he won't wake up. What's wrong with him? Will. *Will.*

She bent down, pressing her cheek against his forehead, stroking his face. She looked up at me.

—Where are we?

—In the house. You had a crash.

—A crash. Yes. I remember. Did you call someone?

—Yes, I said. They're coming. The ambulance is coming. And Mr. Sims.

—When are they coming? My hands are freezing.

—You carried him through the snow. They're coming now.

—Why didn't I wear gloves? she said.

—I don't know. I wasn't with you.

—Where were you?

—I was here waiting for you, I said.

—A crash? But he's all cut up. Look at his face. What happened to him?

—I don't know.

She looked at me.

—He'll be all right, won't he? Do you think?

—The ambulance is coming, I said.

—Yes. The ambulance. That's right. She crouched down on the ground, her hands over her face. I feel dizzy, she said.

I knelt beside her with my knee against Will's leg and held her.

—I hit my head. I can't remember anything. *Don't worry, Ashe,* she whispered in my ear.

—The ambulance is coming soon, I said.

—It's a long way, though.

Car lights shone through the window.

—The Simses are here. Right outside.

—Why are they here? she said.

—I phoned them. I told them to come.

There was a loud knock, and Mr. Sims and his three sons and wife crowded into the hallway.

—Jesus Christ! Sims puffing with a red face.

—Okay. Jane, take Nell into the room. Right there. Nell. Honey. Nell. Please, Nell. Please sit down for a minute. Jane, please go with her. Please. We'll take care of it. You've had a crash. You've crashed your car. I don't know where. Look at her hands. Jesus Christ. Will will be fine. Jane, just take her. Take her, woman, would you! She's bleeding from her nose. Talk to her. Don't let her sleep. Ashe, did you call the ambulance? Mark, phone them again. We can drive him if they don't come soon. Where's he hurt? Let's take his jacket off. Lift him up a bit.

The three men bent over Will. His eyes were sliding around. Sims opened the jacket and bent his head to see the wound. Will screamed.

—*Jesus!* Sims said. Right. Okay. Okay. We can't take the jacket off. Mitch, get some clean sheets and towels. Ashe, where's the linen?

5

I pointed up. Mitch climbed the stairs. He had a full beard and looked older than his father.

—I'll get some water, Ben said, and pushed past me to the kitchen.

—Will, I'm just going to slide you over very gently, Sims said. Will shook his head. Sims pushed him and Will screamed. Sims held his hands up.

—Okay, okay. I just wanted to make it easier for the medics. I'll let them do it. I won't move you.

Will's eyes were squeezed tight with pain.

—I can't find them, Mitch shouted from above.

—Ashe, son, can you help him? We need some towels.

—They said they should be here any minute, Mark shouted from the kitchen. We'll hear the siren.

I walked around the pool of blood on the carpet and climbed the stairs. Will was wheezing.

He'll be all right, won't he? Nell had asked. I hadn't answered her. I noticed myself not answering. Sims wasn't sure himself. Jesus! The way he said it. *Jee-sus!* Trying not to say it, trying not to alarm Will, but saying it anyway, spitting it out.

I showed Mitch the linen closet. I could see Will below through the banisters. I knelt, squeezing the square posts. I couldn't go back down. He stared up at me, ignoring the others, as if it was just the two of us. Sims opened Will's jacket, and Will screamed. Sims covered the wound with a towel as he kept screaming.

—That's okay. That's okay, son. That's it. I won't touch you again. I promise.

Will was crying. Sims sat beside him holding the towel against his side. Will stared up at me, and it was the two of us again. He was calmer. His breathing returned to him. The three Sims boys stood side by side in the hall, their hands in their overalls, looking down at Will with their farmer faces.

—For God's sake, where are they! Sims shouted.

—They're coming.

—Should we take him?

—We can't move him, Sims said. There was fear in his voice.

Will was breathing better now. I listened for the siren. The wind howled and whistled. There. Is that it? Please, please, God, please, the siren, please. Just the siren. Where are they? Please. But there was no siren. Will clutched his throat and coughed up a wad of blood onto his shirt. They tried to hold him up, but he screamed. Blood flowed down his cheek. His breathing was erratic. He was getting worse. I matched his breathing, willing him to inhale, my own body rigid from his struggle, my eyes flooded, his face drifting in bands of light. Will reached for me and I shook my head. No, no. He kept reaching for me, pleading with me, and I kept shaking my head. No, I won't. Then his body arched and twisted, and he slumped down. The men were around him shouting instructions, pumping his chest, breathing into him, yelling over one another, pumping his chest again.

And then they stopped, and Sims was crying, and my mother burst through the door and pushed her way past them. She was on her knees holding Will's face to hers, shaking him.

—Wake up. Wake up. Will. Will. You can't sleep.

And in the distance, between the gusts of wind, I heard the rising wail of the ambulance.

THAT NIGHT, I dreamt of the siren. I plucked it in a field of flowers and put it in my pocket in the bright sunshine when everything was fine. Later, when the storm came and Will was screaming, I wandered through the old house, searching for it, certain it was there, that I'd hidden it somewhere safe and if I could only remember where, everything would be all right. But it was lost, and Will was screaming and wouldn't stop, so I dragged him toward town on the hall carpet, and as I pulled, he kept getting heavier and heavier, and I looked back and I saw it was really Black Rock Park itself I was dragging, its walls plowing through the ground, scraping up the fields of snow, and I couldn't let it stop because I'd never get it going again, so I leaned forward and heaved until I was bleeding from my mouth, and the house began to shake, and I looked around and it was my mother I was pulling, her arms tied behind her back, her body cut and bruised, and I was pulling her by the hair.

2.

The funeral was held in the Catholic church in town. The air crouched hot and still over the congregation as the wind outside rattled the windows. Everyone was there, all the farmers and townspeople. The place smelled of incense and polish and all those country people with their mothball clothes. The women kept looking over at Nell with shiny red faces. She sat next to me saying nothing. She didn't take communion or stand up or kneel. She just sat there staring straight ahead as the service dragged on.

Some old lady was playing the organ. She always picked music with too many notes. A few of the pipes were muffled so the music sounded like it had holes. I was sweating into my wool suit, trapped by the heat and the priest's voice and the endless joyless music. I felt faint when I knelt or stood up. Nell hardly moved through the whole mass. She never even cried. Never. That was the thing. I never saw her cry after the first night. I cried and her boyfriend, Karl, cried and the women in the church cried, but not her. Eventually she did cry, but that was much later.

At the end of the mass, the priest stood in the aisle waiting for Nell to get up. The church went quiet, except for the rustling. When she didn't move, the rustling stopped. Finally the priest walked over and whispered something to her and she got up, and we walked out of the church, everyone staring at us, trying to see in our faces the terrible thing that had happened.

WE BURIED WILL beside my father on a hill in the cemetery behind the church. The two plots were on the eastern slope so they could face the morning sun. Four men carried the coffin up the hill as Nell and I followed. Snow blew from piles along the paths, twisting in spirals, swept around by eddies from the wind breaking over the church and the gravestones. At the grave, I stood beside Nell, facing Karl across the coffin. The crowd stood below us on the hill, looking upward, watching the spectacle of grief, the priest in white vestments reading to the huddled family. And at the centre was the shiny black coffin covered with red roses nodding stiffly in the wind.

AFTER THE PRAYER, Nell stood beside the grave as people filed by.

—We will see you at the reception, Mrs. Finder, the priest said to her.

She said nothing. He touched her shoulder but she didn't look up. He walked down the hill with his head bowed. The people started drifting away. My girlfriend, Sheila, walked up the hill with a white rose in her hand. She was lame in one leg, which made it hard for her to climb up the slope. She went over to Nell and handed her the flower. Nell stared down at it, as if she couldn't understand what

I CARRIED YOU HOME

it was for, then she crumpled it and dropped it on the ground. I took Sheila by the arm and led her down to her parents. I'm sorry, I said to them. They stared up at Nell for a time, then turned and left.

Nell just stayed in the same spot, her eyes shut, her jaw muscles working working like she was chewing something. I stood by a tree to get away from the wind. Karl stayed out in the open shivering, his hands clasped in front of him like an altar boy. The snow started up for a while and then stopped. Why hadn't Aunt Susan come, I wondered. Wasn't she told? How long did we have to stand by the damn hole? It was black from where I stood. I couldn't look at it. I watched Nell rocking gently from side to side, the wind pulling at her dress and hair. Then her knees buckled and she fell face down on the snow with her arms out. Karl ran over and grabbed her under the arms and sat her up.

—Breathe, Nell. You've fainted. Breathe in.

—Don't touch me, she said, pushing him away and trying to get up but sitting down again. She held her hand out to me. *Please.*

I pulled her up, and we walked slowly down the hill, Karl following at a distance. At the bottom she said, I want to drive by myself. You go with Karl.

I sat in Karl's car waiting for her to start her truck just ahead of us.

—I'm so sorry, Karl said, and he clasped my shoulder, and I could feel his hand shaking.

I turned my head away, bracing myself. Don't talk to me, I thought. Don't say anything. Please God, don't talk.

She didn't start the truck and after a few minutes, Karl went over to her window and said something. He held up his hands in submission and walked back to the car.

—She's resting, he said. We'll wait.

The glass steamed up, scattering the streetlights wide. I thought of the faces at the funeral, trying to avoid the image that kept playing in my mind, Will coughing up blood. It had looked like vomit, but then I saw his shirt, and it was blood. And just before, he'd seemed better, his breathing was stable, and I thought he might make it, and it would all be nothing, just another day, something we'd laugh about. But then Will clutched his throat and shook his head and looked up at me. And we both knew it was coming, it was happening. And nothing could stop it now, nothing. Not even the siren. I held my hands out to him through the banisters.

Make it stop, Ashe. Make it stop.

Hang on, just hang on. They're coming.

Make it stop, Ashe, I can't take it.

I can't make it stop. I can't and I won't. I won't stop it.

Make it stop, Ashe. Please.

When it stops, it's over. I won't.

I made a noise and Karl patted my knee. I pushed his hand away and shoved the door open and walked up to the truck.

—I want to go! I shouted.

She started the truck, lighting the field of headstones. I went back to the car and got into the back seat and lay down.

—You okay? he asked.

—I'm sick of waiting.

He started the car and pulled out. He missed the clutch, and we lurched with a grinding sound. He had come up to Nell after the service, his hands held out.

—*Darling, I'm so awfully sorry.*

She'd jerked her head away. *Christ, Karl, I'm burying my son.*

He'd turned and walked off. *You go with Karl,* she'd said to me. The words stung in my chest.

Nell lost us in the traffic and was home first. She locked herself in her bedroom. Karl went up to check on her, and I sat on the stairs, a few steps up from where Will had lain. I didn't look at the floor. I stared at the wallpaper. Then I glanced over, and I saw the mark on the carpet where they'd scrubbed it clean.

Upstairs, Karl knocked on the door.

—Nell. Please. Are you okay? Please.

Don't say please, don't pull at her.

—Nell. Darling. Can we talk?

Don't say darling. She's tired. Leave her alone.

Karl leaned his head against the door, holding the frame.

—I need to know you are all right. Say something.

The grandfather clock ticked slowly beside him. He knocked again, rapping with his knuckles.

—Nell? You won't do anything, will you?

—Ashe! Nell's compressed voice. She was lying face down on the bed.

—Ashe!

—Yes, I called up.

—Get him out of here.

I stood up and looked at Karl and shrugged. He walked down the stairs. As he went by he said, I'm staying over tonight.

I TURNED OFF the lamps in the living room and sat in the armchair behind the television set, watching the light from the screen flicker on the wall across the room. There were two types of crying, one where my face clenched and one where it didn't. They both came and went. I was tired. It was somewhere else now, the thing that had happened. I didn't want it back. I didn't want to think about it, to start it up again, but it wouldn't leave me alone. I could feel it waiting for me, like something staring from the shadows.

When the ads came on, the light flashed in a rush. There's not enough time, the flashing said. Nell. That face she'd made. She had burst into the hallway because of the noise. I saw her when she realized. It took a moment before it sank in. She realized, then she decided it wasn't happening. I could see her making up her mind. It's not happening. There's still time, there's still time.

I kept losing track, watching the flicker. Then I'd see Will's face, and it would all race past me again like I was standing in a river. I tried to think of other things, but the images kept flowing, like the pictures on the television set. I needed sleep, but I had to be tired or I would just lie there. I wanted music, but it was across the room in the cabinet. And there was the hassle of it, the cover, sleeve, turntable, amplifier, headphones. The lowering of the needle onto the spinning groove. It was too much. And the music would play without a break. I wanted it to come and go, with long gaps between the sounds. A bit here. A bit there. Time for the sound to die away and to hear it again in your mind. But not by turning the volume up and down. It should be in the music. It should come and go by itself, like waves on the beach.

Will's room was beside mine. No one had gone in there yet. His bed must still be unmade, the sheets still holding the shape of his body. What else was in the room? I couldn't remember. I wanted to sleep, but it was cold, and there was no blanket. I'd have to go upstairs to get one. I'd have to pass her room. But once you're asleep the cold doesn't matter. I lay on the flickering sofa and pulled the cushions over me.

3.

KARL COOKED HER breakfast the next day with his hair flat at the back where he'd slept. He arranged the food on a tray and waited for the kettle to boil. There was egg down the front of his shirt.

—She's taking it awfully hard, he said. I've never seen her like this.

I didn't look up.

—Of course she is, he continued. Of course she's taking it hard, such a fine boy. It breaks your heart to think.

He could say it that way, in broad daylight, a dishcloth in his hand. *Such a fine boy. It breaks your heart.* As if it could all dissolve into a glass of water, a packet of salt stirred with a spoon.

Karl took the tray upstairs and laid it in front of the door and knocked gently.

—There's some food, if you have a mind to eat. I'll be downstairs.

NELL HAD GONE out with lots of men after Dad died, but at some point she couldn't be bothered changing anymore and she went out mostly with Karl. But that didn't mean she thought much of him.

She'd roll her eyes when he spoke, and she'd cut him off with her hand, and she'd never let him sleep over, though she'd take him upstairs at night and you'd hear the bed squeaking and her muffled groans. She didn't mind Will and me laughing at him, though she didn't laugh herself. She'd just shrug, like the whole subject bored her. She said Karl was tone-deaf *and* colour-blind, which meant he just couldn't understand things, and that was that. Often she spoke to him like he was thick. *No Karl, I don't want to host your office party. Do you understand me? Do. Not. Want. To.* Her voice was softer with everyone else. I wondered how he didn't notice.

I LAY ALL day on my bed. Most of the time I slept. When I woke, I flipped through books of photographs. I looked at the pictures, not bothering with the words. My favourite pictures were of street kids in London in the olden times. The boys looked like little men with their top hats and tattered waistcoats, leaning on each other, cocksure, with twisted mouths. The girls were little women with shabby overcoats and bonnets. There was a picture of a boy and girl in a doorway sleeping together. The boy's head was tucked under the girl's chin. The little brother. I dropped the book. It hit the floor with a double thump.

You had to pass by Will's room to get to the toilet. If you lay flat and still, the urge to pee went away and you could wait longer. He would still be in the room, in the smells of the room. Outside, the snow was pale blue in the fading light. The fir trees churned and twisted in the wind. I could see them when I closed my eyes, the way they moved. I was listening for her all the while. Her bedroom door had a spring lock. It was the same lock on my door. I could hear the sound at will. A grinding metal sound, like the scraping noise in the grandfather clock. But the clock also had a hollow sound that resonated, like when you knock on a piano. When I ran into the house after school and yelled for her and she wasn't there, the clock answered me, *There's no one, there's no one, there's no one.* A mothball sound. Mothballs and varnish.

AFTER THREE DAYS locked in her room she finally ate some breakfast, and Karl said the worst was over, but she refused to come out, and she wouldn't talk through the door and she'd only eat once a day. He waited for a week and then he phoned Dr. Reeves. The doctor came in the evening on the way to a party, wearing a yellow sports jacket and a striped Yale tie. His hair was wavy and lay in a pile across his forehead. He kept running his hand through it like there was a wind, and his moustache was thick and dense with a perfect edge. He would have been handsome—surprisingly handsome—had it not been for a lazy eye that was bulbous and discoloured and always drooped downward, like he was trying to look at your crotch. He'd lean in and pin you with his good eye and tap you as he spoke, and you found yourself bobbing your head with his words, agreeing to what he was saying, trying not to look at his fish eye.

   —This is common, he said. She's had a trauma, after all. It just takes a little understanding. Tact and compassion and understanding.

And time, lots of time. I've seen this type of thing before. I've dealt with it over and over. I'll tell you what, I'll nip up now and have a little chat.

—Would you? There's a master key, Karl said. What do you think? Just in case she won't open the door.

—Good. I'll use it only if I have to, he said.

Karl took the key from his breast pocket and handed it to him. He'd had it ready.

—You can't go into her room, I said.

—Don't fret, Ashe, the doctor said. I know your mother well. We're old friends. I'll just have a quick visit.

—She won't let you break in. She won't let you.

The doctor unbuttoned his jacket and sat down across from me with his hands together.

—Now, Ashe, I do understand your concern. I understand what you're saying, believe me. And I respect it. It reflects well on you. You're looking out for your mother. But I'm telling you not to worry. I'm a doctor. I know your mother well. I'm not her personal doctor, of course, but I've known her a long time. I knew your father too. Did you know that? We were good friends back in the day. I'm just going to talk to her, that's all. Just to check it out. Just a quick chat.

—You can talk through the door. You can't go in.

—I won't go in. Not at all. And if she doesn't answer, I'll just take a quick peek, that's all. Just a glance. Just to make sure she's okay, that everything's fine.

He went upstairs and knocked on the door.

—Nell, it's Dr. Reeves. Gordon. How are we doing, honey? I just want to see how things are going. How are you holding up? Can we talk?

There was no answer. The hall clock groaned and chimed the quarter hour.

—Nell. I know how you must feel. Believe me. I do know. And not just as a doctor. I understand from experience, from my own experience. I'd like to see your face . . . it's important, honey. Can you open up? Please.

I gripped the table.

—Nell, please. I can hear you inside. I have to talk to you. It's no use hiding away from the world. Can you just come to the door?

—He can't go in, I said. She's going to be angry. She'll be very angry. You don't know.

—Just wait, Karl said, holding up his hand. He's a professional. He knows what he's doing. Just wait.

I got up, but Karl put his hand on my shoulder and held me back.

—Just wait, he said, standing over me, looking up at the ceiling.

—Nell. I'm just going to come in for a second. You don't have to get up.

I heard the door unbolt, then a heavy clatter and a piercing scream. Karl and I ran into the hall and up the stairs.

—Fuck! Fuck! Jesus. Dr. Reeves was bent over by her door holding his hand over his mouth, blood between his fingers.

—She hit me! She fucking hit me! There were tears in his eyes. Fucking bitch!

He held his hand out and it was covered in blood. There was blood in his teeth. The cut was in his moustache, the hair had clumped together. I closed the door and stood in front of it.

—I need to see what it was. Fuck it was heavy. Fuck.

The doctor reached for the handle.

—No! I said, pushing him away.

The doctor raised his arm to me, but Karl grabbed him and held him back.

—Come on, Gordon. Downstairs, he said.

—Fucking madhouse. Fucking lunatic. I don't care, Karl. I don't care what she's going through. All over my jacket.

—Come on.

The doctor pushed Karl aside and walked downstairs by himself, clomping on his heels, his hand over his face. The key was still in the keyhole. I bolted the lock and pushed the key under the door and sat on the top step. I could hear Karl talking in long sentences. I couldn't make out the words, but it was all sympathy. The tap was flowing in the sink. The doctor was washing himself. He'll call the cops now, I thought. I imagined a pair of policemen pushing into her room with Dr. Reeves behind them.

Karl came out into the hallway.

—Is there any antiseptic? he said.

I went to the bathroom and found a bottle of rubbing alcohol and brought it down. Karl went back into the kitchen, and I sat on the lowest step. The doctor roared, and I stood up, then I realized it was the alcohol stinging his lip. He'll have to shave it off, I thought. I went to the hall closet and took out an umbrella and stood at the bottom of the stairs. I heard the doctor leaving through the back door. A car revved hard and drove down the driveway.

Karl came out into the hall.

—Do you have the master key? he said. He was angry—not embarrassed, actually angry.

—No.

—Where is it?

—I gave it back to her.

—But why? For God's sake, child, why? Why would you do that? It's the only one there is.

—It's hers, I said. It's her key! It's her house!

—Calm down, kid. Calm down.

—It's not yours, I said, pointing the umbrella at him. It's not your house. You're not married to her.

—Christ. Thanks for the bulletin, Karl said, and then, Fuck.

It was the first time I'd heard him swear. The doctor had started him off. He stared at me with his hands clenched. I stood with the umbrella held up like a sword until I felt foolish and dropped my arm.

—We're in for it now, he said. He'll go to the police. And he'll sue. I know that guy. He's a vindictive bastard.

—You brought him here.

—Fuck.

He leaned against the door frame. He still had some egg on his shirt. He slipped his watch off his wrist and stretched it around his hand. It had an elastic gold and silver band. He kept snapping it against his palm.

—He'll tell everyone. Just you wait. Everyone. The goddamn provost of Yale will know about it tomorrow. And he was going to some big party. They'll all find out. He'll make sure everybody knows why precious Gordon didn't show up. I'll hear about it at the office tomorrow, I guarantee you that. Christ. He said he was going to the hospital. Everyone in the hospital will know. Why did she do it?

—I told you. I told you not to open the door.

—Did you see what it was?

—That American thing. That statue of hers, the torch woman.

—The Statue of Liberty. That figures. That's your mother all right.

He started tidying his hair.

—Look, I'm going to the hospital. Maybe I can calm him down a bit, maybe it will help. He's vicious. You wouldn't know it the way he carries himself, but I've seen how he gets. I'll go down and help out. I'll have to talk to his girlfriend too. Fuck.

I took my father's coat from the closet and lay down on the living room sofa with the coat over me, the collar against my lips. I could smell something under the mothballs, the faintest of odours hiding in the cracked leather. Not perfume. Cologne ... my father's cologne.

4.

KARL WAS OBSESSED with the estate where we lived, Black Rock Park, a great Victorian mansion far out in the countryside. We lived in one of its smaller wings, the old servants' quarters, walled off from the rest of the house. The main part of the house was empty and falling to pieces. It was too big to fix and too broken to sell, so we were trapped there; we couldn't leave without abandoning the place. Nell hired men to patch up the walls and roof and worried about the house crashing down on us some stormy night, but most of the time it was just there in the background. And we hardly noticed it. Someday, we'd walk away and leave it to the mice.

But for Karl, Black Rock was something else. He loved everything about the place; he'd hunt through the city archives and law reports for clues about its past; he'd talk to the older farmers in the surrounding districts, digging up bits of gossip here and there. He'd amuse himself for hours with his notebooks, putting the pieces together like it was a big puzzle to be solved. *It's not in bad shape, really,* he'd say, striking the wall. *The structure's still sound, after all these years.*

24

I'd watch him taking groups of friends around the grounds, lec-
turing about the history of the house, how it once had five hundred
acres and was filled with the finest furniture and paintings money
could buy. *Twelve palatial suites, he'd say in full oration, a music room,
a solarium, a two-storey library, a ballroom, and a banquet hall, every pane
of glass, every wall panel, every wood beam fashioned by a master craftsman.
Such a house belonged in the richest neighbourhood of the richest city, not in
the hinterland with cows and snowdrifts. So how on earth did it end up here?
This isn't England after all. We don't have feudal estates here. Who would
build such a house in the middle of nowhere?* He'd look into their eyes,
and then with a flourish he'd pull out a picture of the great man in
a top hat.

*Stanley Gerald Fitzroy, he'd say. One of the leading industrialists of
the nineteenth century, and one of the great socialites and clubmen of his day.
He'd lived his whole life a city block from the stock exchange, but then a great
change came over him in his late forties. One day he runs an empire and the
next he sells everything off, jumps a ship and travels around the world with a
dog and a single leather suitcase, and when he returns, he builds this fortress
for himself as far from people as possible. But why did he change, you're asking yourself? What came over him?*

Karl would lean into the group and point at someone and say
quietly, *Nobody knows. Nobody! But an old farmer around here once told
me a strange story. He was the grandson of Fitzroy's old grounds manager
and he said that Fitzroy told his grandfather something odd over whisky.*
The group would murmur and crowd forward. *He told him he woke
late one day with a cold and had to race across town and run upstairs to
make a board meeting, and while it was going on, he was restless, and he*

walked around the long table and looked out the window at the building across the street, at the pattern of light on the wall, and he saw it flicker, like it was under water, and he fell to the floor. Then he was looking up into the faces above him and he saw something flash through their eyes. Malice, he said. Cold steel malice, pure and simple. It made his flesh crawl. He was defenceless, and they were all huddled around him. He was at their mercy. It was ten against one. Then he recognized their faces and remembered the meeting, and he thought, have they done this to me? Was it something in the water? Did they lace the water? And then the moment passed, and he knew he'd just fainted from a fever and nothing had happened. He got up and went home. But he never forgot the look in their eyes. He never trusted them after that . . . This was the story he told the grounds manager that night. And we know that shortly afterwards, he sold everything and travelled around the world. And when he came back, he took a simple housekeeper for a wife and built this house and locked himself away.

It was a good story, and I'd have believed it myself, if I hadn't heard him tell an earlier version where Fitzroy was a captain in India lying wounded on the ground, and a group of soldiers were huddled around looking down at him with malice in their eyes, and that was why he'd turned against the world. So it was all made up. Karl couldn't find the real reason, if there even was a reason.

But the rest of the story was true enough. The house took five and a half years to build, and Fitzroy constructed a small town near the site to house all the engineers and artisans shipped in from around the world to build it, and when it was all done, the town was dismantled and the land restored, so the house looked like it had sprung from nowhere, and people coming up the road would stop and stare at it, as if seeing something truly amazing, an Arctic iceberg floating in a summer lake.

Then many years later, Fitzroy's son lost the family fortune in the great market crash and had to sever the servants' wing from the rest of the house with wood partitions to make it through the winter. He lived alone in the truncated house and survived by selling off furniture and fixtures, and in the end he sold the whole estate to a carpenter for next to nothing. The carpenter built proper walls in place of the partitions and boarded up the rest of the house and went on to buy a broken-down furniture factory to match his broken-down house.

And that carpenter was my grandfather, a lowly tradesman from Ireland with grandiose dreams who inherited a sum of money from a rich uncle at a time when the entire country was going bankrupt. He set out to make his mark on the world, but somehow nothing worked out for him, and he ended up burnt-out and bitter and eventually died when he was still young. Without wanting to, my father inherited it all, the mansion, the grounds—at least what was left of them—and the furniture business. He was studying to become a painter after returning from World War II, but suddenly there was no one to run the business, so just like that, he was making rocking chairs and collapsible tables to survive, living in Black Rock Park, the house that should never have been built.

And now Karl wanted it for himself. He wanted to be part of the story. He probably dreamed of restoring it someday and throwing parties there for all his law school friends, regaling them with tales about Stanley Fitzroy, *his* brilliant, eccentric ancestor.

K<small>ARL WAS STAYING</small> in the house every night now. His files were stacked on the kitchen table, and he kept bringing over more and more things. He invited my mother's sister, Aunt Susan, to stay and help with Nell. I was scared of her. She was insect-like, tall and skinny, with wide sculpted shoulders and a sinewy neck, and she wore tight clingy dresses so you could see her nipple bumps. Her face was bony and pale with a few faint freckles around the eyes. She used powder and bright red lipstick, which made her look like a geisha girl. She was four years younger than Nell, but her stiff manner made her seem older. She'd always pause before smiling, and she'd say, That *is* funny, instead of laughing.

She was a high school teacher and lived alone in a big city in a basement apartment. A few months back, she'd come over for dinner, a casual summer meal, which she ate with perfect table manners. She listened to Will and me with a tight smile, nodding too much as we talked, as if she already knew what we were going to say, so we found ourselves tapering off at the ends of sentences. I thought she was strange and somewhat grand but nice enough, until I met her alone in the hallway.

—What grade are you going into? she said in a dead voice.

—Ten.

—Ten? And how old are you?

—Fifteen, I said.

—Fifteen? How did you do last year?

—I did good.

—You did *well*, not good, she spat. *Good* is an adjective. *Well* is an adverb. Do you know what an adverb is?

—It's when a horse marries a cow and makes a goat, I said.

—You're an ignorant boy, and you'll be an ignorant man if you're not careful. A lonely, ignorant man.

I went upstairs to the washroom and sat on the floor in the dark. What had I done? Why did she hate me? I couldn't remember saying anything to her. I hadn't even looked at her at dinner. Was that it? I felt shy looking at her, knowing Nell didn't like her. *You'll be a lonely, ignorant man.* But she was the lonely one. She smelled of it. All that perfume. A lonely heart. She hated being lonely. You could tell from the way she said the word. Her basement apartment was dark with fake wood panelling and stained linoleum floors and a smell of piss from the baseboards where cats from a previous tenant had sprayed. She'd washed them over and over, but the smell wouldn't go away. I imagined her on her knees in the dark with a wire brush scrubbing the shredded boards.

I asked Karl how long she was staying.

—For a while, he said. Until we get a maid. She's taken a leave of absence from her teaching job. We're very lucky she can help out.

—Mom doesn't like her, I said.

—Why do you say that?

—Because she told me. She's always saying it.

—She's said a lot of things, hasn't she.

—She didn't invite her to the funeral, I said.

—She forgot, she wasn't thinking.

—But she hates her.

—Oh, now she hates her, does she? I wouldn't worry about it, Ashe.

He turned and walked away.

5.

AT DINNER, SUSAN was getting on with Karl, laughing at his lame stories, calling him an honest-to-God character, accusing him of honeyfuggling the natives, refusing his praise for the lasagna, saying it was too dry and tasteless, hardly edible. And Karl was puffed up like a winter pigeon, bolting down the creamy pasta, a dribble on his chin wandering as he talked. He explained about the house and the neighbourhood as if he'd lived there all his life. Red-faced with excitement, they both ignored me, Karl looking Susan over when her eyes were down, staring at her nipple bumps, plainly visible in her tight white dress, Susan reaching over and tapping his hand as she talked, playing up to him. They were sitting there because of Will, but they'd long forgotten him.

—Get some more water, would you, Karl said. He pushed the jug at me, not waiting for an answer, continuing with an old story about a farmer client of his who'd worked a parcel of someone else's land for years by mistake and was so angry when Karl told him he had to stop, he burst into his office with a pitchfork demanding to know how much blood money he'd been paid.

When the meal was nearly over, Karl asked Susan about Nell.

Had they always been close? Always. Had they ever fallen out? Never. Were they still close? Extremely, if only schedules and distance would allow them to spend more time together. At the end of the day, family was all there was. Karl agreed. Family was the whole ball of wax. So you are *good* friends. Yes, yes indeed, the best of friends, a touch on his hand. I can get through to her, a twitched smile, a squeeze on the wrist.

Karl looked at me pointedly.

—You can clear the table before you go, he said, showing Susan who was boss, though he'd never have dared talk to me like that in front of Nell.

—You should have seen Karl, I said. He got this doctor friend to come over to look at Mom, and the guy just barges right into her room and she nails him with a statue, right in the face, and there was blood everywhere. Everywhere.

—She's very angry right now, Karl said in his lawyer's voice.

—No. It's her room. The door was locked. You gave that guy the key. I told you he shouldn't go in. You wouldn't listen to me.

Karl looked at Susan and shook his head.

—You think you know what's going on, don't you, Ashe, he said. Susan was shaking her head back.

—I know that if the doctor sues, you should pay for it. And I know something else. I know something you don't.

—That's all right, Ashe, he said, holding his hands up in mock surrender.

—I know what she has in that room.

—That's all right, boy, calm down.

—She's got a gun, I said. So I wouldn't try it again.

—I've been in her room hundreds of times. She doesn't have a gun.

Hundreds of times. The only time he went into her room was at night when they rattled her bed. It was hundreds of times, he was saying, that's how many times I've done it to her.

—She doesn't have a gun? Really? All right. If you say so.

—As if Nell could be dangerous, Susan said.

—No? You should have seen that guy's face. You finished? I picked up Karl's plate, which still had food on it and dumped it in the sink.

—I was eating that, Karl said.

I grabbed the plate and shoved it back at him. The lasagna rolled onto the table.

Susan held up her hand.

—Don't worry, Karl. I know about Ashe. I know all about Ashe. It's a terrible loss we've had, but we can't have people acting out with Nell in this state. We have to think of her first. Things will have to change around here.

—You know how they used to get rid of witches? I said.

—Tell me, she said.

—With fire! *Whoosh!* I raised my arms.

—You threatening me, boy?

—The floors here are wood, aren't they? Sometimes bad things happen to big houses. *Whoosh!* I slammed my hands on the table and she jumped. Karl got up, but she held him back.

—That's okay, she said, straightening her dress. You'll see, Ashe. Just wait. You'll see.

—I don't care. I know about you too. You can't get a man because no man will have you. No one will put up with your sour face. You poison them, that's what Mom says. You're a sour old maid. And you! (I pointed at Karl.) You're not supposed to stay here overnight. No one invited you. It's not your house. It'll never be your house. You're just one more boyfriend. She'll dump you like all the rest.

I knocked the jug over on the table and left the room, slamming the door as the water spilled onto the floor.

Lying on my bed I could hear them through the air ducts, their urgent voices rushing in streams, Susan punching every fifth or sixth word, laying down the law, Karl following in a deep grumble, agreeing with her—as far as she went—but adding more, because she was too kind, his tone said, too lenient, too forgiving.

Sour old maid. She'd looked at Karl at those words, trying to get his reaction before he covered it up. Just her eyes moved—I saw the veins in the whites—then they swung back at me and struck me. *This is serious,* those eyes said. *I'll hurt you for this.* I imagined her standing over me as I slept. What would she do? She'd think of something. She'd teach me a lesson, something nasty. That was certain. I got up and locked the door.

They were talking slower now, pausing before answering, enjoying their outrage. I imagined walking into the kitchen with a gun and pointing it at Karl. *Look what I found, Karl. I told you it was there.* But I had no gun. Nell wouldn't let us have guns, no air guns, no cap guns, nothing. They teach boys the wrong thing, she always said. But she didn't care about that anymore. She wouldn't even talk to me. She'd carried Will for a mile through the storm, but to me she had nothing to say.

I remembered that Will had matches in his bedside drawer. They were in a wood box, hidden at the back, hundreds of them, and not safety matches but plump, fizzy matches with red-and-white heads that you could strike on your shoe. I unlatched my window and pulled on a sweater and went into the hall with a flashlight, locking my bedroom door behind me. Karl had his loud voice on, telling some smartass story he'd told a hundred times before, pretending it was the first time, rattling on about pea-brained farmers. I paused by Will's door. I didn't want to go inside. I didn't want to smell his room or see his things frozen in the hall light. I pushed the door open and rushed over to the bedside table and rifled through the drawer until I found the box of matches. As I turned, I saw the unmade bed and remembered Will lying in the hall. I bent over, holding my head. It's over now, it's over now, it's over now. Then I smelled the room, and my face clenched, and I knelt down. It's over, it's over, it's over, I thought, trying to shout down his face, trying to bully it away, so it wouldn't keep saying: Can I go now, Ashe? Can I go now?

I left the room. Susan was laughing downstairs. There was a light under Nell's door. I took a match from the box and went downstairs and listened outside the kitchen. Karl was talking about how *splendid* the town was and how *sterling* the folks were, but that he shouldn't have come back after law school. He should have stayed in the city while he was still young. Susan said big cities could be lonely if you didn't have family there. Karl said that was true, very true, but he didn't sound like he believed it. He talked about his law school classmates and the big practices they had.

I went down to the basement and lit the match and held it to the wall until the wood blackened, then I blew it out and pressed my cheek against the mark, watching the smoke from the match streaming upward. It was so easy to do. Why hadn't it happened before? The building had been falling apart for years. Everywhere the wood was dried and cracked. All it would take was one match. I turned on the flashlight and went to the back of the basement and opened the fuse box. I flipped the main switch down, shutting off the power to the house. Karl yelled upstairs. I unscrewed the six fuses and put in some blown ones from the shelf above the fuse box and blackened the casings with a match so it looked like they'd blown in a surge, and then turned the main switch back on. I hid the rest of the fuses and ran outside through the basement door and around the house and climbed up the latticework, pulling myself onto the roof and crawling back in through my bedroom window. I changed into pajamas and got into bed. Karl was shouting downstairs. He couldn't find a light. I laughed under my blankets though it didn't seem at all funny.

After a minute, Karl stomped upstairs.

—Ashe! Ashe! This is not a joke! Where the hell are you? He rattled the doorknob.

—Ashe! Open up!

I opened the door and he shone a flashlight in my eyes.

—What did you do? he said.

—Nothing.

—There's no power.

—That all? That always happens.

He pushed past me into the room and looked around.

—What did you do? Did you fiddle with the fuse box?

—No, I was sleeping.

—Do you know where it is?

—It's in the basement somewhere.

—Well, come down and help me find it. His tone was softer.

—I don't know where it is, I said. Mom knows.

—You won't help me?

—I've no idea. Mom knows.

—Jesus Christ!

He left the room and knocked on Nell's door.

—Nell, I need to find the fuse box. Nell. Nell! Can you tell me where it is?

He put his ear against her door for a moment.

—Goddammit! he said, smacking the wall. He marched downstairs.

I locked my door and lay down. There it was. She wouldn't come out. Not for any reason.

6.

I WAS SHIVERING in the dark. I looked over at the window expecting it to be open but it was closed, then I remembered changing the fuses. No power meant no heat, the gas couldn't burn without electricity. I could see my breath in the air, like I was outside. I kicked off the blankets and pulled on my clothes and went downstairs.

The fridge was open, and the light was off. The food was outside on the porch in a cardboard box, frozen solid. I ate some rye bread and an apple and went out into the cold and took my bike from the garage and rode down the gravel driveway, the great house gliding beside me in the gloom like a ship pulling out of port. The roads were empty, not even the farmers were up. I raced with the wind at my back. I worked up to tenth gear, spinning fast. Everyone was asleep, and I was tearing downhill, falling, flying. Then the wind hurt my face and I rode slower with my head down.

It was light by the time I got to school. I sat outside the front door with my coat pulled up over my head and my aching hands between my knees. There was a knock at the window behind me. It was Mr. Chung, a cigarette dangling from his mouth. He opened the door.

—Why you here? he said.

—I'm early.

—Okay then. He stubbed his cigarette on the ground and put the butt in his pocket.

—Can I come in? I said.

—Wipe feet. Why you here?

—I'm the new principal.

—Okay then. And don't mess. You hear? I clean.

I sat on a bench as he mopped the floor.

—I no smoke, you hear? he said over his shoulder.

—I know. I don't care.

—I no smoke, he said again, glancing at me.

—I won't say anything. I—won't—say—anything, I said, holding my hand over my mouth.

—Okay, okay, he said, but he looked unhappy.

—Don't tell the teachers I came early, I said.

—Wha?

—Don't—tell—teachers—I'm early—today. Okay?

—Don't tell? he said. Okay, okay. Forget, I don't say. He wiped the floor again, but he looked happier now he had his surety. The furnace kept whirring and clattering, starting up and shutting down. The air was too hot. I took off my coat and opened a window. I noticed it had a spring lock that latched in the sill. I found a pencil in my coat, sheered off the eraser, and jammed it into the lock and closed the window so it looked like it was latched.

—I can mop, I said.

—Wha? No. No, he said, shaking his head.

—I can mop. I'm good. I flexed my muscles. I'm strong.

—Like this, he said. Do like this. He swept back and forth and rinsed out the mop in the bucket. I took the mop from him and did the same.

—Good. I watch.

I washed the floor in long strokes, cleaning the salt prints from the tiles. After a while, he walked off. He had a dragon tattoo on his arm and gold around his teeth and a deep scar under his eye that dug into his flat nose. I often watched him from the classroom, trimming the hedges and mowing the lawn and picking up the garbage, always with a cigarette between his lips. It bobbed up and down when he mumbled, ash falling on his shirt. I'd wait for it to fall.

I finished the hallway and left the mop and bucket in the washroom. Mr. Chung was vacuuming the classroom up the hall. I stood by the doorway watching him. He pointed to the blackboard and said something in Chinese. I went over and erased the board and tidied up the desk and put the books back on the shelves. When the room was done, he held the small of his back, groaning in Chinese. We went on to the next room. He chatted to me in his language as we cleaned the room. He was complaining about something. It was the same tone he'd used about his back. When we finished, he put the vacuum away, and we sat on the stairs by the main door. He hummed a tune with three long notes as we looked out the window.

—Eight, he said, tapping his watch. Go now. Teachers here soon. Come back at bell.

I went outside and walked over to the graveyard. Up the hill, the snowcapped gravestones all looked the same. I threw a stone at a grave, and a bird took off and flew up the road and over the clustered trees, bare and twisted, that marked the end of town. I sat against a tree and waited. The wind was stinging my face, cold, cold wind, like ice water, like acid. I didn't think about Will, about how he was up there on the hill, thrown away. I thought only about the cold, and how I'd be warm when the school opened, and how the heat would make my fingers ache and itch. When the bus arrived I walked down to the schoolyard and went inside with the other kids.

AFTER SCHOOL, I rode to King Street and wandered around the stores to stay warm. I bought a bag of shelled peanuts and ate them on a bench, flicking the shells over a snowbank. When it was dark, I rode back to the school. There was a car parked in the driveway, but all the lights were off. I hid my bike in a bush and walked around the building, checking the rooms, but there was no one there. I went to the window I had rigged and pried it open with a stick and climbed inside. It was the main hallway. I tried the classroom doors but they were locked. One of the handles wiggled, and I shoved it hard, and the door snapped open. There were little tables and chairs everywhere and the smell of glue and fingerpaint. The kindergarten. A line of stuffed toys hung from pegs on the back wall, one for each child. I lay on the ground with my coat bunched under my head.

Hot stale air was blowing from the vent. Something rattled from the corner. I jumped up with my arms out and saw the glint of a wire wheel. The pet mouse. I watched the wheel turn, pause, turn.

I put the cage on the ground and lay down beside it. The mouse was quiet for a while, then it started running again. I watched the street lamps through the cage wires and the spinning wheel and the streaked window and the tree branches. One light was slightly blue, one was yellow. I stared at them until the lights blurred. The blue light was fluorescent. A dead colour.

WHAT DOES SHE think about, lying there? Does she think about Will? Does she think about anything? Maybe she just floats, drifting in and out of sleep. But Will won't leave her alone. He keeps waking her up. I haven't gone, he's saying. Look around you. I'm in everything, my face, my voice, my body. I'm mixed in. You'll never get me out.

Part of her knows he's gone, part of her doesn't know. His face keeps appearing. Surely that's him. Surely. Who else could it be? Who else could be behind that face? I can see it moving. It's not me that's moving it. You'd know if it was you. Look at him, that expression, that very look of his. He's holding his peace. It's him exactly. See. He knows something, but he won't say what. And you'll never drag it out of him. Not Will, not when he's like that. But he's not like that. It's not him. I'm sorry. It's just a puppet you're seeing. Are you lying to me, boy? I can feel you're here. You're behind me, aren't you? No? You are near, though. You're downstairs somewhere. You're in the hall. Are you still in the hallway? Did you never move from that place? I can hear you breathing. It was all a lie—all that carry-on—a naked lie. Admit it. You know it's the lying I hate. Don't ever lie to me, boy. You hear me? Your endless lies. There's nothing wrong with you. You were tricking me all along. It was just a cruel prank, wasn't it. Let's scare her half to death. Let's see what she does. Well, now you know.

What ever happened to that old Finder woman anyway? Is she still lying there, day after day?

I remembered lying beside her on her bed. The room was hot from the morning sun and the smell of flowers and perfume and her body. A window was propped open, and a stream of air trickled over my feet. The bed was covered with patches of red and yellow from the stained-glass panel propped in the window. We listened to piano music on the record player. We talked about this and that, I couldn't remember what, maybe her life when she was a girl, how she stayed outside every day in the summertime until dark, climbing the trees and playing in the fields and looking after the blind billy goat with milky eyes. That was before her mother died when she was eight, three years older than I was when my father died. As she spoke, lying on the bed, I watched the tangled shadows on the ceiling and thought about my father. I would drift in the heat, and I'd feel him in the room somewhere, perhaps in the music, in the bass notes, coming and going like the sound of voices when you wait for sleep. I remembered walking with him on a white beach. He held my hand as we went into the water. Schools of tiny fish—no bigger than ink drops—weaved and darted through my legs, angry seagulls cried overhead. He picked me up and threw me in the air and sat me on his shoulders. I was scared of the barking gulls. They'd attack me from the sky. I kicked and screamed and my father took me down and we waded through the water dragging a toy boat upside down in the waves. My father was the first to leave. Then my brother left. They were together now, side by side on the hill, listening to the same wind I was listening to. They were lying there day after day, the way I lay beside Nell.

You could feel her whenever she was near by. It was like she carried a big room with her, wherever she went, a huge space that was silent and still and surrounded you both. I'd chat to her about everything and anything, the great big world outside, what was wrong with it, what was right with it. She'd lean forward in her chair, nodding slowly with her eyes wide open, absorbed in what I was saying, like I had the key to some puzzle she wanted to figure out. The best thing was sitting with her after running out of things to say, just sitting there, not needing to say anything. You felt fine just staring out at the trees to the lopsided beat of the grandfather clock. Other people pecked away at things all day— this this this, that that that—and you had to keep thinking of things to say back, but not her. She was quiet and unhurried. She'd smile slowly and reach over with her long elegant fingers and ruffle your hair. Now and then, she'd give you a sly look, and you knew exactly what she meant, she didn't have to explain it to you. We'd go outside and lie on the grass and watch the birds overhead, and she'd tell me to be quiet and watch—just watch—just see what you can see—and we'd stay there so long I'd close my eyes and start drifting off in the wind. There was nowhere to get to, and nothing to be done.

But there was another side to her. She didn't like us bringing friends to the house. Country people pry into your business, she said. You have to stay on your guard. But then one summer I went to a party and met Sheila Meegan, a girl I'd seen around but never talked to. She lived a few miles from us and went to a different high school. I used to ride by her farm to catch a glimpse of her. Once she was standing by the road and she brushed her hair from her eyes and my limbs went weak and heavy. Then someone took me to a party and, without even trying, I was sitting next to her and she was talking to me and we spoke for hours, and then she called me up the next day and asked me to pick apples with her on her farm. I was burning to show her off to someone. I brought her over to the house without telling Nell first. We sat at the kitchen table and Nell sat across from us and hardly looked at her, just glancing over at her at intervals, as if on a timer, trying not to be obvious. I had to speak for the three of us. When Sheila got up to straighten her dress, Nell gave her a long puckered stare. Then, after a few minutes, Nell excused herself and went upstairs to make a call. We waited for her to come down, but she stayed upstairs. I went into the kitchen and picked up the phone but there was no one on the line. I told Sheila there was something Nell had to deal with, and took her outside to see the house.

Afterwards, Nell said, She's quite a bit older than you, isn't she?

—Only ten months, I said.

—She looks a *lot* older than you. Very . . . you know . . . very *mature* and all.

—Well, she isn't.

After a long pause, she sighed and said, It's a shame about her leg. Such a nice girl. So pretty. So sweet. I'm sure all your girlfriends will be nice.

It was easy to miss—*all your girlfriends*. It meant, this isn't the right one. You have to keep trying.

Later, I told Nell about Sheila's father, Mr. Meegan, a farmer who talked and talked like he knew everything, but when you argued back, he'd laugh and listen to what you said and even change his mind. You couldn't help but like him.

—Maybe Will and I should marry Sheila and her sister and become honest-to-God farmers, I said. Real cowpokes, how about that? I'm serious. We could turn Black Rock into a massive farm with cows and pigs and tractors everywhere. Can you imagine? We'd get good ol' Mr. Meegan to teach us how. He'd love that, training a pair of rookies from sun-up to sundown.

She raised her eyebrows and looked down at the floor.

—Farming? she said. Is that what you're thinking now?

—No, I'm just joking. I'm not serious.

—You sure?

—Hey, it wouldn't be so bad. You should see Mr. Meegan, he's as happy as a bird. He loves everything. He talks a blue streak all day long. Even when he's by himself on his farm. He's pretty funny.

She looked up at the ceiling and her eyes narrowed.

—Sheila Meegan . . . so that's what this is all about.

—No, it's not, I said. I'm just talking. It's called shooting the shit, Mom, that's all. It's nothing.

—Once you were going to be a sailor, remember. Like Joseph Conrad and Herman Melville, you said. You were going to run away

45

to see the whole world, see everything there was, until you were full up. You didn't trust anyone telling you about it.

—I know.

—*Sheila Meegan?* Really?

—What's wrong with her?

She smiled.

—She is a lovely girl. But she said it slowly, staring at me, like it was a test and I had to say the right words to pass.

—She's all right, I guess. I mean, she's just a farm girl.

—No, she's very pretty.

—I guess. She's nice, though.

She leaned forward and put her fingers together.

—Ashe, you don't want to lose that instinct of yours, that impulse you have, being Joseph Conrad and roaming around the world and all that. Anything can happen in your life. *Anything.* That's so important to remember.

—I won't lose it, Mom.

—I don't want you to *limit* yourself so young, you understand me? I'm not trying to restrict you in any way, I just want you to think big while you still can. I want you to stay open to things.

—I know. I'm not limiting myself. We just . . . I just met her, that's all.

—She is lovely, I grant you that. So graceful and shy. I understand why she fascinates you.

—She doesn't fascinate me. *Jesus*, Mom. She's not even my girlfriend. I just met her. She asked to see the house, that's all. I'm pretty sure she likes older guys anyway.

—Of course she does. We're all seeking experiences, aren't we? Lots of experiences. And that's what you're looking for, Ashe. That's what it's all about.

She started tidying the room because the conversation was over, as far as she was concerned, but it was like I'd agreed to something I didn't want to. I was suddenly angry.

—What's wrong with Sheila and Mr. Meegan? I said. Why can't we just be the same as everyone else? Just nobody, anybody? Why can't we just be happy like that?

She stiffened, carefully laying her hands on her lap.

—You'll find things out as you grow older, Ashe. Her voice was deep and measured, and my heart was beating fast.

—It's a long, hard road you have to walk in this life, she said. Don't limit yourself is all. There's more to find out, things you don't know about yet.

—What's wrong with the Meegans anyway? What's wrong with ordinary people? Why can't I just be like anybody?

Her nostrils flared. She crossed her legs slowly.

—Think carefully, Ashe. Before you decide anything now. Think very, very carefully, that's all I'll say.

—What does that mean?

—It means don't close yourself off. Don't decide anything now. Just wait and see.

—I'm not deciding anything. I'm saying something different. I don't understand why you're always so mean about people. They're just people. Why do you hate everyone? You hate the whole fucking world, Mom!

Then she gave me a look—*her* look—a dead-eyed stare that froze your blood. It's hard to explain. It hurt you when you saw it. It wasn't hatred exactly, it wasn't contempt. It was a hint of something much worse than that, something permanent. A type of banishment.

—Of course, I still want to see the world, I said, and go to university and learn things and all that. I'd never stay here, for Chrissakes.

She looked over my head, like I might not be able to convince her this time.

—I'm not going to be stuck here like everyone else. No way.

She nodded slowly.

She *is* a nice girl, she said. A nice *first* girlfriend, shall we call her that? A *practice* girlfriend, think of it that way. There'll be many more.

—She's not my girlfriend, I said. You don't have to worry. I just met her.

—You're an intelligent boy, Ashe. You understand what I'm driving at. Your sympathy for people can be used against you, without you ever realizing . . . Nice people with problems, nice people with difficulties beyond their control, no fault of their own. That's all I'm saying to you. Don't get trapped by these people, even if they're very, very nice. Okay?

—Yes.

—Okay. She is lovely, though. I'm glad you brought her over. Can you put your things away now? I have to get dinner on.

So according to Nell, Sheila wasn't going to be my girlfriend. I wasn't allowed to have her, this ordinary girl who intended to trap

48

me. But I tell you, I'd never heard anything so fine in all my life, to be trapped by a beautiful girl like that, a girl who wanted to steal me away from Black Rock and everything else. I'd never thought of it that way, this hidden desire in ordinary girls. I wanted her to be up in my room right then and there. I wanted to lie on my bed with her on top of me, staring into my eyes with her hands on my shoulders and her full weight on my belly. What else was there to want?

7.

IN THE EARLY morning, I got up and left the kindergarten and went outside and rode into town. The streets were quiet with new snow. A woman was standing at the bus stop on the main road. She had a scarf wrapped around her head and was staring at the empty lot across the street. I stopped pedalling, and the *whirr* from the freewheel made her turn toward me. She was young with a pale face and bright red lips. I felt her watching me. She'd be wondering why I was there so early. I rode over to the diner and glanced back. She was staring at the lot again. I leaned my bike against the window and went inside. It was empty except for an old couple in the corner sitting with their coats on. I sat at a table and watched them drink their coffee without looking at each other. They're married, I thought, nothing left to say.

An old waitress came over.

—You by yourself, son? She had cigarette breath. She was thin and bent over at the shoulders. The skin under her chin hung loose and wobbled.

—I'm waiting for my mom, I said.

—Is she eating?

—No, she's just picking me up.

—So what do you want then?

Everything was old in the restaurant, carpets, tables, menu. The light bulbs were yellow, one of them winked on and off with a ticking sound.

—The breakfast special, I said.

—How do you want your eggs?

—Scrambled. And some coffee, please.

—How old are you? she said.

—Fifteen.

—You got money?

—Here. I showed her the cash in my wallet.

She brought me the coffee.

—Why are you out so early? she said. Why are you by yourself?

—I was staying at a friend's house and we had a fight.

—A fight? What about?

—A girl. He said I stole his girl.

She laughed and sat down across from me.

—And did you?

—No. She just likes me. It's not my fault.

—Don't drink that, she said. I'll make you some tea. The coffee's far too strong here.

She was someone's mother, you could tell. She came back with a teapot and some milk.

—It's not good for you that, she said. The caffeine. You're still growing. He makes it like tar.

—It's okay, I said, but she was right, it tasted burnt.

—You have brothers or sisters?

—No, I said.

She looked out the window and shook her head.

—We shouldn't open so early. We're the only ones open. No one comes in at this time. He won't listen to me. She nodded toward the kitchen. I'd just as soon sleep. Oh, here they are now. Here come the boys. Marty! They're here!

Two policemen pushed through the door, pulling in the cold air.

—Gentlemen, gentlemen, good morning, she said.

A fat man in an apron came out from the kitchen.

—Arnold. Brent. Anywhere you like.

They sat in a booth across the restaurant from me. One of them was older and had a bushy moustache. He stared at me before opening his newspaper. The waitress brought my food and I ate quickly, not looking directly at the policemen but watching them from the corner of my eye. I asked for the cheque.

—You haven't finished already, have you? she said. You in a hurry?

—I have to meet my mom. I don't want her to wait.

She gave me the cheque. The policeman with the moustache got up and came over to my table.

—Hi. I'm Arnold, he said. Mind if I sit down? The table jerked as he sat, spilling the tea. He looked out the window, scratching the stubble on his chin.

—Where are you off to today? he said.

—Nowhere. I'm just eating.

—Don't you think you should go home?

I didn't answer.

—You're Ashe Finder, right?

I stared down at the cheque, at the way her letters looped.

—Karl Hodges phoned me last night. He's a friend of mine. He said he was worried. He said you didn't come home last night.

I traced the loops of ink with my finger.

—Don't you want to go home? he said.

I shrugged.

—Look, kid, you have to go home, I'm sorry. My partner and I are having breakfast, then we'll give you a ride home. You want to sit with us?

I shook my head. The waitress came over.

—He said he was waiting for his mother, she said, showing her allegiance.

—It's okay. She asked us to pick him up instead. Here, I'll get this. He picked up the cheque. Put anything else he wants on my bill.

The waitress watched the policeman walk back to his table.

—You in trouble? she said.

—No.

—You sure?

—Yes.

—You want anything?

—Coffee.

She brought me a cup of coffee and some cake.

—You might as well, she said, he's paying. What did you do?

—Nothing.

—Want some ice cream?

—No thank you, I said.

—It's Italian. It's very good. I'll get you some.

She brought some green ice cream in a bowl.

—Don't look like that, try the cake. He made it himself. She nodded to the kitchen. It's good. He bakes it at home.

I took a bite.

—See? He swirls the toffee inside so it's not dry.

—Do you know Karl Hodges? I said.

—Karl. Sure. He comes here for lunch. Everyone knows Karl. Why? You done something to Karl?

—No.

—He done something to you? she said.

—No.

—Why'd you ask about him?

—Nothing, I said. He's dating my mom, that's all.

—Is he really? she said. I know Karl well. He do something to you?

—No, he's fine.

—Yes, he's a *lovely* man. He bought me a watch for Christmas, look. She showed me a watch with large numbers.

—He noticed I couldn't read the clock, so he bought me this watch. Imagine that. He only sees me at lunchtime, and he remembered.

Three construction workers came in, and she went off to seat them. I looked at the empty booths where Karl sat every day beside the grimy window in the sour bacon smell, polishing his glasses with his tie before reading the menu he knew by heart. He gives her a watch and she tells the whole town. He was no fool. He had his own way of getting by. You'd see him in town playing the big man, winking and waving and patting folks on the back. He was liked. Everyone smiled when you mentioned Karl Hodges. That's what he was most proud of. It's what he had instead of a wife and kids. Of course, it was all an act. You only had to look in his eyes to know how lonely he was. You'd walk into a room and catch him off guard, and he'd have this hangdog look like he was about to cry. But instead of going out and getting a wife, he was chasing after a woman who didn't care a damn about him. And for some reason he couldn't stop himself. He had to impress her. His stories always had him doing the decent thing, helping some rube farmer he could just as easily screw, though he'd say it in an offhand way so it didn't sound like he was boasting. He'd laugh at his own weakness for a good sob story, saying how hopeless he was, how he'd never had a head for business. Then he'd flash his dopey grin at Nell, not expecting praise exactly—the smile was embarrassed and shy—but hoping for something at least, longing for it. But she never gave it to him. She'd just raise her eyebrows and change the subject. We all knew what he was up to. And now he had his big chance. Before the accident, he used to lounge around, groaning whenever he stood up, but now he paced about, rarely sitting down. And it wasn't worry about Nell or anything like that. It was his good luck bubbling up inside him.

The two policemen got up from the table. The other one was squat and muscular with a shaved head. He was a lot younger than his partner. He held his hand over his gun as he walked, chewing a toothpick.

—Come on, he said without looking at me.

The construction workers turned and watched me leave. I sat in the back of the police car. The younger policeman got into the passenger's seat, as the older one put my bike into the trunk.

—So where were you last night? he said in a policeman's voice.

—Nowhere.

—Nowhere? Don't lie to me, kid. Where did you sleep?

I didn't answer.

—Your mother phoned us twice last night and twice this morning. We've had four calls for you. What were you doing last night?

—My mother phoned? You sure it was my mother?

—She phoned four times. Are you trying to scare her to death? What were you doing?

—Just riding around, I said.

—Yeah, sure, in minus fifteen.

The older policeman got into the car.

—Okay, my friends, Black Rock Park.

—He doesn't know where he was last night, the younger one said as we drove up King Street.

—Lay off, would you, the older one said. I told you not to start.

—I'm just saying.

—Leave him alone.

The younger policeman shrugged.

—Just saying.

But I felt warm all over as we headed out of town. Nell had phoned four times. I watched the ice melting on the heated filaments of the back window. She was up; she was worried. A great tide would flow back now and wash Karl and Susan and everything else away, and it was only fair. They wouldn't try to argue with her. My God, they wouldn't dare. Nobody crossed Nell when she was angry. She was stronger than any man. I remembered Mr. Purser, Dad's business partner, striding up to our house after Dad died, with his tweed suit and pinched face, how he talked with Nell for a long time in the sitting room until it was just her talking, and then she was shouting at him, and he scurried out without looking at me. He'd come on behalf of the minority shareholders to offer her a pittance for the controlling share of Dad's furniture business. The situation was dire, he said. We'll have to find a new manager, and probably won't make a profit for at least a year, seeing as we've just lost the only person with any know-how or connections, but our biggest concern right now is *you* and your two young lads, that you don't take on any undue risk in your new circumstances. We couldn't live with that on our consciences. But Nell didn't fall for it. She knew he was spooked and wanted to sell the thing off as fast as he could, so she did the unimaginable for a housewife, she found a buyer herself and struck a deal, and in the end they all went along with it, the price was so good, though Mr. Purser told everyone she'd gone behind his back and made it sound like she'd cheated them somehow. That's how she saved us from ruin. We didn't have to scrape and beg. We had all the money we needed. But Mr. Purser stayed furious at her. Years later, he cursed Nell in some social club Karl belonged to, and Karl was hopping mad.

—I'll straighten that man out, he shouted.

—There's no need to get red in the face, Nell said. What did he say, for God's sake?

—He called you a name I can't repeat. He'll think twice before he does that again, by God.

She laughed.

—Did it start with a *c* by any chance?

—He'll pay dearly for it, I promise you that.

—Is that all it was, Karl? Why get so excited? Lord love him. Such a funny little clot of a man. A country shopkeep, through and through. He hadn't a clue what the business was worth. He couldn't understand the name my husband had made for himself and his designs. He'd have sold it for scrap. I made him more money than he'd ever dreamed of. So of course he's mad. He tried to cheat us and I outfoxed him. He'll never forgive me for that.

Karl stared down at his drink, swirling it around, his face burning, all his fine words wasted. She didn't give a damn about his chivalry.

KARL WAS STANDING at the door when we pulled up to the house.

—Stay here for a minute, the older policeman said. We're just going to talk to him.

The two policemen walked over to Karl. He looked sheepish, his head bowed, his hands deep in his trouser pockets. He didn't look up at me. They all went inside the house. Surely Nell had sorted him out. But where was she? I looked for her in the windows but she didn't appear.

The policemen came outside. The younger one took my bike out of the trunk, and the older one sat in the front seat.

—Okay, my friend, you can go now, he said.

—Where's my mother?

—She's sleeping.

—But she phoned you, right?

—No. It was your aunt that phoned.

—The other guy said it was my mother.

—I took the calls, not him. He doesn't know who phoned. They've all been worried sick about you, son.

—Sure they have, I said.

—Look, it'll get better. Don't take off, because we'll just have to find you again and buy you breakfast. It's a waste of time. Just stick it out. Okay?

I said nothing.

—At least wait for spring. How about that?

He was looking at me through the rear-view mirror, a pair of tired eyes in folded skin. He seemed old without his moustache.

—You can sleep outside in the spring. It's a lot easier. You'll freeze your balls off now. Okay?

I nodded.

—Right. Off you go.

I got out and the young policeman handed me my bike and jabbed my shoulder with his thumb.

—See ya soon, kid, he said.

~~~~~~~~~~

SUSAN AND KARL were waiting in the hall.

—Where have you been? Karl said.

—Nowhere.

—We didn't know what happened to you, he said. Anything could have happened. You can't just take off like that.

—I'm going to bed.

—Why did you leave? At least tell us that, Susan said.

—No reason.

They were standing in front of the stairs, blocking my way.

—We have to talk about this, Karl said.

—Why? I shouted. Are you my dad now? Is that what you told the cops?

He stepped aside. I brushed by him and went upstairs. The policeman with the moustache must have said something to him. He had no fight left. I looked down over the banister. They were hidden in the hall shadows, standing beside the fern plant, its leaves brown and dry, with the ends clenched like fists.

—Where's Mom? I said.

—In her room, Susan said.

I knocked on her door.

—Mom! Mom!

There was no sound. I knocked harder, shaking the handle.

—Mom! Let me in.

I dropped to the ground.

—Answer me, I said quietly. Say something, at least.

I lay flat on the floor, my face against the gap, feeling a stream of air on my eye. I remembered her pulling me as a kid. She was taking me to a fair, just her and me. I was very young and didn't want to go. I was scared of the big boys pushing and shouting, and I wanted to leave, but she persuaded me to go on a spinning-cup ride. She smiled at me as the ride turned around, sure I'd be laughing soon, but my cup wouldn't spin. I shook it furiously, trying to set it free so I could laugh and she'd be happy, but it stayed stuck, and when I walked back to her, she looked disappointed. Then she bought me a bottle of Coke and I dropped it on the ground and it poured into the trodden dirt and I cried in the middle of the fairground in front of the big kids. She picked me up and took me home. In the car I was certain she would be sad forever, that I could never make her happy. I remembered that exact feeling, the Coke forever spilled, my mother forever sad.

—Mom.

—I can't, she said quietly, without intonation, without sadness.

I imagined her face, implacable and hard. I got up and kicked the door with the toe of my boot.

—Fucking bitch! You fucking bitch!

I pounded the door with both fists, trying to break it down. Then I stopped, and the house was silent again, the noise swallowed head and tail. The grandfather clock ticked beside me. I hit it with my palm, and it clattered and chimed, and the pendulum tangled in the wires and stopped swinging. As I walked to my room, I could hear the clock ticking in my mind. Looking over the banister, I saw the two of them, Karl and Susan, standing in the same place, ready to talk.

8.

In the evening, I heard Karl and Susan laughing downstairs. They'd spent all day together. I was thinking about riding into town to get some food when someone came upstairs and knocked on my door.

—What is it? I said.

—It's Susan.

I opened the door. She had a drumstick in a mug.

—I cooked some lemon chicken. Try it, she said, holding it out to me.

—No thanks, I said.

—Go on! It's good.

—I'm okay.

—Will you come down to dinner?

—I don't want dinner.

I tried to close the door, but she put her foot in the way.

—It'll be in half an hour, she said.

I lay down on my bed. My stomach started up and I thought about the chicken, its crispy skin, its roasted-lemon smell. I went downstairs and the three of us ate together. Susan was attentive.

Would you like more potatoes? Is that the way you prefer your chicken? I could fry it if you want. The onions are underdone. Leave them on the side.

I was polite in return, thanking her when she served me. Karl smiled placidly and said very little. It was a truce.

THE NEXT DAY, Karl brought home some wine. Susan said she didn't drink, but Karl insisted. A rich client had given him a case of Chardonnay. She had to try it, at least. He poured her a glass. She drank it quickly and then took another without protest. Her arms loosened and her hands waved and she forgot about me and chatted busily with Karl, her cheeks and chest a mottled pink. Karl said the rich client relied on him for everything, from planning his parties to ordering his clothes.

—He's had a valet his whole life, he said, and he comes to me last week with his hair standing up and his shirt buttons in the wrong holes, and he says his man's as sick as a dog, what should he do? Which of course meant one thing. Yours truly.

—No.

—Yes indeed. He was helpless, absolutely helpless. He doesn't trust anyone else.

—You mean you dress him yourself?

—Yes ma'am, every morning.

—You're not serious.

—I certainly am. He can't dress himself. He gets all flustered if no one's there to help him.

—So how do you do it, how do you dress a rich man?

—First you shave his face nice and smooth, then you comb his hair flat, then you help him into his clothes. It's not hard. We always start with the socks. And at the end he's so grateful. It's heartbreaking, really. Susan, have some more. It won't keep. You must. We'll finish the bottle.

—I'm hot, she said, fanning herself.

—It's good for you. It's good for young women. Doctors say that.

—Which doctors?

—Doctors with stethoscopes. It gets the blood flowing. It airs you out. You can feel it, right? Oh, and I trimmed his eyebrows today.

—No, you didn't.

—I surely did. They were immense. You should have seen them. Epic eyebrows. He looked like a crackpot. I didn't even ask him. I just combed them out and snip, snip—Bob's your uncle. He didn't say a word. He looks much better now, poor sod.

THAT NIGHT SUSAN couldn't sleep. She walked up and down the hallway outside my room. I lay listening to the floorboards creak. She was mulling things over, trying to decide something. I remembered locking the door, but was that today or yesterday? She'd hear if I checked. She'd know I was up, that I was listening to her. Then it would be the two of us together in the dark. I imagined her bursting in with a knife, screaming like a tribesman. Would I have time to roll clear?

I woke in the dark with a full bladder. The creaking was gone. I shuffled across to the door. It was unlocked. I crept along the hallway to the bathroom and knelt in front of the toilet, peeing along the porcelain so the urine flowed around the bowl instead of raining in the middle. I left it unflushed and was walking back to my room, pulling up my underwear, when I saw Susan. She was standing with her back to me looking out the window into the bare woods. The morning light shone through her nightie. I could see her woman's body under the silk, her curved buttocks joined in a dark cleft. She turned and looked at me with her arms crossed, and then she dropped her arms, and I could see her two nipples through her nightie like two eyes and her dark patch like an open mouth.

—Well? she said, as if I was supposed to do something.

I dropped my head and turned into my room. She made a noise as I closed the door, a quick exhalation, like puffing out a candle. I stood in the dark, listening for more. Was she laughing at me? I lay on my bed with my hand over my eyes, my face hot, thinking of her laughing at me with her black cleft. That dark, dark cleft, darker than any shadow.

IN THE SCHOOLYARD the next day an older boy smiled at me and said something under his breath. I stepped toward him and hit him in the face with my tight fist, right against the cheekbone, snapping his head sideways, and then I stood there with my arms by my side looking straight into his twisted face, taunting him, surrounded by a sea of gobsmacked children, and the boy struck me hard across the windpipe, and then I was down, trying to breathe, feeling for my Adam's apple. I am killed, I thought. And then Mr. Maude was shaking me, and I could see the brush hair in his nostrils and smell his pipe breath and I heard him saying, Fayn-der! Fayn-der! with his Irish accent.

Uck you! was all I could manage, and I kicked Mr Maude's backside with my boot and felt the toe glance off the bone just as my fist had glanced off the boy's face, and then I was pulled up by both arms, Mr. Maude's thumbs digging between the muscle and the bone, and I was dragged past the children in the schoolyard through the hallway into the principal's office. The boy followed us and stood at the door.

The principal was mortified, pushing back into her chair as if trying to get away from me, the lines on her chicken neck hidden by her tweed suit buttoned to the top.

—I have seen some *vicious* boys in my life, she said with a shake in her voice. But just look at that child's face!

And there he stood on display, tall and fat, tears running down his cheeks, a purple eyelid swollen shut, innocent as the day is long. Don't cry for her, I thought. I looked down at my shoe in the silence. A splatter of mud on the toe looked like an island in the sea. She kept staring at me, trying to get me to talk. I wiped the island away with the toe of my boot, grinding the grit into the leather. Keep staring at me, bitch, you can't make me talk.

She sent me home for a week, and the old bus driver drove me in his car without saying a word, and when I arrived, Karl was standing there at the door with the same dumb expression he'd sported since his girlfriend locked herself away. Don't pretend I'm your son, I thought. But when Karl saw my face, he bent down and said gently, What did he do to you?

—He said, *Will is a ghost.*

THAT NIGHT, I went down to the basement and pulled aside the sheet of wood that covered a hole in the wall between our house and the old mansion. Will and I had made it once with chisels and a pointed saw so we didn't have to keep going outside and around the house to get in. I squeezed through the hole and felt my way along the main hallway and into the ballroom. I lit a candle and shielded the flame from the draft that blew steadily across the room. When the flame took, I dripped a pool of wax onto the floor and stuck the candle upright. If I fell asleep, and it tipped over, the whole house would go up in flames, burning in a pile, streaming ash and embers across the night sky.

—Will, I said. *Will . . .* you there?

The flame fluttered but hung on. Outside, the wind gusted, howling over the roof, streaming through the gaps in the walls. A branch hit a window with a sharp clack. My head jerked backward and struck the wall. I smelled smoke. The flame was out.

—Will! I shouted.

In the darkness, the tears were fingers tracing down my face. I slumped down on the ground, my arms over my head.

I WOKE AT dawn with an image of the ember glowing in the dark. It had stayed lit a long time after the flame blew out. I watched it until it died and then closed my eyes and watched the reverse image until it too was gone, sinking backward into nothing. The flame was Will, I thought. And the ember was Will too. The ember was Will lying in the hall.

I went back to our side of the house and up to my bedroom and slept in my clothes. When I got up, Susan was downstairs. I wandered into her bedroom and looked through her things. She had black lace panties. You could see your fingers through the weave. I held one up to my eyes and looked out the window at the white trees. One of the trees had blown over in the wind. Its black roots were showing. Was there a smell in the fabric, under the detergent? Her smell, trapped in the dark seams. Crotch. I threw the panties down. Yesterday I'd caught a whiff of underarm when she reached by me for a plate, an animal smell, hiding in her lace shirt, in the soft places she'd forgotten to wash.

The floor creaked outside. I dropped to the ground and crawled under the bed. She came into the room and closed the door and lay down. She threw her shoes and stockings onto the floor.

—*Jesus* Christ, she said.

I held my breath, listening to her squirm and settle on the bed.

—They all think that, she said.

I was lying awkwardly on my arm. She would hear if I straightened it out. My hand went numb. I watched an ant crawling across the floor, feeling its way through the balls of dust. Shadows from the branches of a tree grew slowly along the wall like vines. After a long time, her breathing was deep and regular. She mumbled and flopped around.

—Up the mountain, she said. No, up there. Three times. No. Four. Look at it. Please, yes. (Her dream was busy. She was striving with people.) Another one please. On top! On top! Yes. Yes. Drop it there . . . Maybe a lemon one . . . Hold it in the light . . . a lemon sash.

From the hall, the clock struck the hour.

—What? she said. Jesus.

She got off the bed and her dress fell to the ground, then her shirt and bra and panties. She was standing in front of the mirror. I stretched over to see. She was facing away from me with her arms up. She turned and I saw twin shocks of tufted hair under her arms and a patch of clotted hair below with a black line tracing up her belly. Her nipples were brown and textured, the size of dollar coins. They looked pasted onto her pale skin. She started to dance, slowly at first, then faster and faster, humming as she moved. I felt her heels through the floorboards. Nell had told me that Susan had wanted to dance for a living but didn't have the nerve to audition for a proper academy. She danced for close to twenty minutes, then stopped. She stood in front of the mirror breathing hard, sweat rolling down her belly, beading on the dark fingers of hair. She stroked herself up and down.

I inched back from the edge of the bed, as far as I could go. She rummaged through her suitcase across from me. I could see her eyes. She only had to look around and she'd see me. She stood up and plugged something into the wall and lay down on the bed. There was a buzzing noise. She was shaving her legs. Why didn't she shower first? My nose itched. I squeezed the sides savagely, breathing through my mouth. The tickle went away. She started to grunt at intervals like she was lifting a weight. Was it hurting her? My mother used shaving cream and a razor after a bath. It didn't hurt that way. The bed rocked gently back and forth. The grunting grew urgent, a steady release of tension straining from her throat. It went on for a few minutes until she gave a stifled cry, and the bed was still. It wasn't shaving. It was something else, something private. I didn't know women did it too. And in the middle of the day. Like she was dying for it, like she couldn't wait. She lay still for a while, then she got up and dressed and went downstairs. My own aunt. My mother's sister. She didn't even wash. Wouldn't you wash after that? Then I thought of her soaping herself in her black cleft. My own aunt. If she'd caught me, what would she have done?

THAT NIGHT SUSAN opened the wine before Karl got home and drank as she cooked. She wore lipstick and a white silk shirt buttoned low. When Karl arrived, she put candles on the table and turned off the lights as if they were a couple eating alone.

—Just use your hands, she said, putting a plate of spareribs down. She ripped the meat with a twist of her head, leaving red stains on her chin.

—You can go to school tomorrow, she said.

—I have to stay out a week, I said.

—I saw your principal. You can go back.

—You saw her?

—I went down there and talked to her.

—What did you say?

—I just told her what that boy said to you. She wasn't surprised. She thought it must have been something like that. She knows he's mean, the little shit. I wasn't going to let him get away with it. She called him in and asked him what he'd said, and he swore up and down he'd said nothing, that you just went for him. Then she asked a few of the kids in his class, and they all said they'd heard him saying it and that he laughed about it afterwards. So now she knows. I had my own little chat with him in the playground, just the two of us. He won't bother you anymore.

—What did you say to him?

—I told him I'd rip him apart if he did it again. Not in those words, of course.

—You threatened the boy? Karl said. He might complain, you realize that.

—I didn't threaten him, Karl. I just told him the plain truth. I said if he mentioned Will's name again, I'd gut him like a deer.

—You said you'd gut him?

—Something like that, she said.

—I know the Bullions, Karl said. I do work for his father. He's a big client of mine.

Susan looked up, sucking on her thumb.

—I told that little shit about what people used to do to boys who showed disrespect for someone else's loss. I told him that sometimes they strung them up, sometimes they ran them through, sometimes they just shot them to save time. *Bang!* And not just the person who showed disrespect, but anyone who defended that person. And I told him if he wanted me to explain it to his parents, I'd quite happily go over there any night and tell them straight to their faces.

—You threatened the boy. You realize that, Karl said.

—I explained things to him, that's all.

—You shouldn't have scared him. I'll hear about it now.

She threw a bone down on her plate.

—I don't care if you hear about it, Karl.

—Well, it's done anyway. No point going over it. It's a great meal. Isn't it, Ashe?

—Bullion's a bastard, I said. He likes hurting people.

Karl pushed his chair back.

—You hit this boy in the face. That's hurting someone, isn't it? I've never hit anyone in my life.

Susan laughed.

—I believe that, Karl. I really do.

We ate in silence. Susan stretched past Karl and took the wine bottle.

—You should see his eye, she said. You did that with one punch?

—Yes.

—Show me.

—Like this.

I punched the air, twisting my fist.

—It's red and yellow, she said, a thousand shades of yellow, like a flower. It's beautiful, really.

—I don't think you should encourage him, Karl said.

—I'm not encouraging him, Karl. I'm congratulating him. It was Bullion who encouraged him.

—We'll talk about it later, he said.

—No, no we won't. There'll be no talk later. She took a long drink.

—Don't you think you've had enough? he said.

—Who is this man? she said to me.

—Her tenth boyfriend, I said.

—Ten boyfriends. Imagine. I do think she picked the best one, don't you?

—I won't be insulted, Karl said. I won't just sit here and take it. I'm here helping Nell.

—You want an award for that? she said. Is that it, Karl? We're all helping her, but she's not eating, is she? She's hardly eaten for two days. She told me to fuck off today. I said, Please Nell, please let me in, and all she said was *Fuck . . . off*. Like that. Like it bored her just to say it.

—She'll come around. It takes time, Karl said.

—So says the boyfriend, she said.

—The doctor told us to give it time.

—Is that the one with the statue in his head? she said. Do you mean that doctor?

—Maybe I should just go, Karl said. I mean, is it even helping, me being here?

—I'm her sister, Karl.

—What does that mean?

—It means I'm not deciding whether or not to go. For me, it's not an option.

—I can't say anything right, now, can I, he said.

—There are no rules, Karl. Just do what you think right.

—All of this because I criticized you? Because I said you shouldn't threaten a boy?

—No, Karl, that's not it. All of this because you weren't angry. You didn't get angry. You didn't even feel the insult.

—I know it was insulting, he said.

—You know it, but you don't feel it. That's the difference.

Karl sat for a while looking out the window.

—God knows, I've been patient. I've tried and tried. All I've ever gotten from this family is insults.

—Poor Karl, she said, smiling at him, touching his hand.

—Why is that, Susan? Why is it this way?

—Don't you know?

—No, I don't.

—It's because you're the outsider, Karl. No one likes the outsider.

9.

IT WAS THE middle of the night, and someone was tapping at my door. Susan, I thought, lying still. The tapping continued. It wasn't going to stop. I got up and put my ear against the door.

—What is it?

—Open up.

Nell. I opened the door, and there she was in a winter jacket. I reached for the light, but she stopped me.

—I can't start the truck, she said. The battery's dead. How do I boost it?

—Where are you going? I said.

—Can you come down and help me?

—So you need my help now?

—Shh! Keep your voice down. I don't want to wake them up. Can you help me?

—Where are you going? I said. It's dark outside.

—I just need to go somewhere. Will you help me or not?

I stepped aside and she came into my room. I turned on the reading lamp. She stood against the wall. Her hair was oily and tied back in a knot. She watched me as I dressed. I put on my jacket and found a flashlight.

—Do you have jumper cables? I said.

—I don't know.

—Do you have Karl's keys?

—No, she said.

—Then how are we going to boost it? We need the keys.

—Hang on.

She switched off the reading lamp and opened the door.

—He'll wake up, I said.

She went over and turned the door handle slowly and went inside. The light turned on. I waited for Karl's voice. Then the light turned off, and she came out with a set of keys. I followed her downstairs.

—Where are you going? Can't you tell me? I said.

—No, I can't.

—It's freezing out there. The truck might not start.

—It'll start all right, she said. Don't worry.

—How do you know?

—It'll start.

—Can I come with you?

—No. Sorry.

There was a gym bag on the kitchen table. She picked it up and we went outside into the cold. I climbed into the back of the truck and looked through the tool box.

—There are no cables, I said.

—Karl will have some.

We checked his car, but there were none there either.

—Damn it, she said. The garage.

I pulled the door open and turned on the light, and right above the bench was a pair of jumper cables hanging on a nail.

—That's them, right? she said.

—They're rusted up. They won't work.

—Here, she said, grabbing a file from the table. File the ends.

I filed the teeth until the metal shone.

—They're okay, I said. They'll work now.

—Of course they'll work. Come on.

She started Karl's car and moved it in front of the truck. I opened the two hoods and connected the batteries with the cables. I sat in the truck's front seat and turned the key. There was a clicking sound. I tried it again, but it was dead. She can't go, I thought. She can't go. Nell came over to the window. I turned the key. This time the engine turned over a few times and stopped.

—Do it again, she said.

—I think it's dead.

—No. Just don't turn it all the way. It's diesel, remember. Turn it halfway and let the plugs heat up. When that light goes off, turn it all the way.

I'd forgotten there was a trick when it was cold. I did as she said, and the engine started easily, a cloud of black smoke rising behind us.

—Where are you going? I said.

—Come on, get down. I have to go.

—Take me with you.

—No, she said. I can't. I told you already.

She opened the door and pulled my arm to get me off the seat.

—What's in the bag? I said.

She held it behind her back.

—What is it?

—Come on, she said, pulling me harder. I jumped down.

—What about Karl's car?

She handed me the keys.

—Just leave it where it is. It doesn't matter.

She got into the truck and closed the door.

—Are you going to visit someone? I said.

She looked up at the sky.

—There's no moon tonight. Did you notice? That's why it's so dark.

—What time is it? I said.

—Late. Three something.

—So are you going to visit someone?

—Yes. I'm going to visit someone, she said.

—You should stay. You should go tomorrow. The roads are bad.

—I have to go. Let me see you. She turned on the cab light and looked at me. She brushed my hair back.

—It never would sit down, she said, and turned off the light. I just wanted to see you. Wipe your eyes.

—Why do you have to go?

—I have to, that's all.

—Go tomorrow.

She reversed the truck to get around Karl's car. I held on to the side mirror. She drove forward, and I ran beside her for a few steps and then let go and watched the truck driving down the white lane to the road.

I went upstairs to her room. The door was unlocked. In the corner was my father's army chest. I checked the box at the bottom. The gun was gone.

10.

THE STORM HAD been blowing for hours, knocking the wicker chairs up and down the porch. Out by Highway 16, a transmission tower had toppled in the wind, cutting the power lines, strewing live cables across the road. We were huddled together in the living room, a circle of candles on the coffee table. Susan was curled up on the sofa, holding a glass of wine, letting the red drops settle before taking a sip. Karl was stretched out on a rocking chair, staring at his shoes, twisting them about so the dabs of light played on the leather. I was lying on the chaise longue, looking around at nothing in particular—him, her, the glass, the shoes, the flames. I listened to the shutters flapping against the windows, waiting for the heavy slaps that, hours ago, had made us all jump.

—They're sure to fix the power tonight, Susan said.

—No, they won't, Karl said. It's the main line that's down. It'll be tomorrow morning at the earliest.

—At least the phone works.

He picked up the receiver.

—Not anymore, he said.

She ran her finger around the glass making a thin wavering

note. The candlelight cut across her face. When she stopped smiling, her face collapsed, showing another face, the one she'd have when she was old, crossed wrinkles, sunken hollows, pinched corners. I was scared of that face. I distrusted her new-found friendliness. It wasn't for me. It was for someone else, a mistake she'd made. She'd find out soon enough, and then she'd blame me for it.

—How long since she left? Susan said.

—Four days, almost five, Karl said.

—Where the hell is she?

That pointless question.

—She's just gone somewhere. She wants to be alone for a bit.

It sounded flat this time, like he didn't believe it himself.

—I mean, what else could it be? he said. It's been four days.

His words weren't quite veiled. It's been four days. If she'd done something, he was saying, we'd have heard by now. He covered himself with a blanket and leaned back to sleep. Susan was staring at the film of wine on the glass. I shut my eyes so she wouldn't start talking to me.

Nell was out there with a gun. It's the hardest thing to do, I thought. The hardest thing. For anyone. To arrive at that final moment. No more minutes left. No more seconds. Right now. With no pause between doing it and feeling it. Not like poison, where there's still time. And in that final moment, to find the strength to pull the trigger. And it would be hard for her to pull because of the rust. The first pull was never enough. You had to pull a second time, much harder, your hand ready for the extra tension. Who could do it twice? And after all it's been four days.

Four long days. And then it flowed the other way. But where is she? Why hasn't she phoned? If you cocked the gun first, it was easy to pull the trigger. She might have done it already and they haven't found her yet, her truck parked in some empty field. That look of hers when she was leaving. Detached, like the world was not her concern, like it was already behind museum glass. I just want to look at you, she'd said, as if she was going away for a long time. Maybe she wanted to go for good, but she couldn't, because it's the hardest thing to do, even if you want to. Harder than anything. I was walking around the hole, calculating the odds, all the strands pulling toward the hole, all the strands pulling away. Standing at the edge without looking down, without thinking what it would feel like to fall into such a hole. Thinking was a waste of time because she wouldn't do it. It was the hardest thing to do. She wouldn't be able. But where was she? Why hadn't she phoned? And so it went, around and around.

—The kid asleep? Karl said.

—Yes.

—Hey, Ashe.

—Don't, you'll wake him.

—*Hey*, Ashe! You up?

—Leave him be. Let him sleep.

—Just checking. That's the last of the wine by the way. Just so's you know.

—That's fine.

—I thought you didn't drink.

—I didn't, she said. Where is she, Karl?

—I don't know, I don't know. Would you stop asking me that? Nobody knows except her. That's how she wants it.

—But where could she be?

—She's in a hotel somewhere. She's lying in bed in a bathrobe, eating room service, watching TV with a towel around her head.

—You think so?

—I don't know, do I? he said. You keep asking me.

—Will she do something to herself?

—No, of course not. Then after a moment, *Who knows?*

—The question is, Susan said, would she ever do something to herself, could she?

—You can't tell what she'll do. That's one thing I know about Nell. She's not like other people, not like anyone else I've ever met. I was thinking about that just now. How we once went for a walk across this wooden trestle, this old railway bridge, about two hundred feet up, with rocks down below, and Nell walks right along the edge, all the way across. Right on the edge. One little slip, one puff of wind, and she'd have fallen.

—Was she angry about something?

—Probably. She's always angry about something, isn't she? You know her. *You don't understand me, Karl. No one understands me. I'm all alone in this.* That sort of thing. But it wasn't any more than usual. There were these big gaps between the planks, and the wood was uneven. She could have tripped easily. I mean, I tripped myself, walking beside her.

—But afterwards, what did she say?

—She didn't say anything. She wouldn't talk about it . . . You sure he's asleep?

She bent over me.

—Ashe? she whispered.

I could smell her wine breath.

—He's asleep. I can hear the way he's breathing.

—He hates me enough, crazy kid. If he heard me talking about her, he probably *would* burn the place down.

—Still, it's amazing to me the power she has over men, she said. She whips you and insults you and turns you into this nice little boy, and you just put up with it.

—You think it's like that, do you?

—I know it's like that. I've seen you with her. You've lived inside it so long, Karl, you can't see it anymore. You think this is just the way she is, but she wasn't like this with Patrick. They were best friends. They were always laughing and teasing each other. She wasn't angry or desperate or cynical. She was happy. A different person entirely.

—So it's me, is it? he said. I'm the problem?

—No. It's not you, it's her. It's her problem all right. She gave up. She settled. You're just something she owns, Karl. You're an appliance. I'm sorry to say it like that. It sounds cruel, but you don't know her like I do, who she once was, what she really lost, why she's so angry. We've always fought, the two of us, but we understand each other. We're connected, despite everything. That makes you smile, does it?

—Well Susan, you have to realize, I've heard her talking about you. Even Ashe told me she hates you.

—You've no idea, do you? You've no idea, yet you argue. You're that sure of yourself, and you can't even stand up to her. I asked you what she said after walking on that bridge and you said she didn't say anything. That's because you didn't really ask her, did you? You didn't *demand* an answer. Tell me, over the last four days how many times do you think she's thought about you, precious Karl? How many times? Because I guarantee you she's thought about me. There are just a few people that come into this—Ashe, Will, Patrick, and me—her real family. What about it, Mr. Hodges? Do you think she's thought about you much?

—You tell me, he said.

—You're not even there. You don't exist. She's told you that many times, but you can't hear it.

—So you blame me for what's happened, do you?

—No. It's not you. How could it be you? You're nothing to her.

—You're both the same, you and your sister. You're both miserable in the same way. You're beaten down. You're like a couple of convicts in jail, convinced you'll never get out again. You keep going over it in your head, how you're trapped, how you'll always be trapped. But I think it's a lot easier than that. You decide things, you let go, you move on. You drive your truck down the road, and every so often something precious drops off the back and smashes on the ground, and you're sure you can't live without it, but you keep on driving, don't you? You keep on living. The world unfolds. A new world. Different from the past, different from Patrick, not in conflict.

—It's that easy, is it? she said.

—If it's worth anything, it's that easy. You and I, right now. We could be different. We could drop all of this, forget everything we know about each other, about ourselves. I'm not the enemy, Susan. I might be an outsider, but I'm not the enemy, for Chrissakes. We're allies at the very least, fellow travellers. Friends, I hope. I mean, am I the enemy?

—No, she said.

—Well then.

—The problem is, I know how this all ends. A cop shows up and tells us the bad news. I know it.

Karl got up and sat beside her. I wanted to look over at them. Susan was crying. Karl was comforting her. They were whispering. Then they went quiet, and I heard a rustling noise, like they were moving about on the sofa.

—No! Susan said.

—I'm sorry, I'm sorry.

—No, not here. Ashe. *Upstairs.*

—You sure? he said.

—Upstairs. Quick. Quick!

They went upstairs together. I lay listening to the storm, the liquid sounds, the beats, the strands, the voices. Under the noise, that one note. I could hear it blowing. The one note that said, nothing is yours, nothing is for keeps. I remembered learning that for the first time, the shock of it, trying to contain the fact, to put it somewhere, that everything will be nothing, and the nothing that everything becomes is like static, like the snow on the television set, formless, with a rushing sound. And the nothing is hiding all the time behind everything, the way winter storms hide in the summer, hide in the noises of the river and the shaking leaves and the whipping fabric sound of wind rushing past your ears. It's hiding there all the time, ready to rise up, ready to roll across the land and sweep everything away.

I climbed the stairs. They were in Nell's room. I lay beside the door and listened to Susan making those guttural sounds she'd made on her bed, sharp releasing groans, evenly spaced, pushing from her throat. But they were different now, fierce, taunting, spurring. She was talking to Karl with the grunts, urging him on, thanking him, praising him. I listened until she cried out, then I went downstairs and lay on the sofa.

It was over. Nothing had happened. I was empty. Whatever it was, they'll say it happened in a storm. The things you do in a storm never count for much. But on my mother's bed. Whose idea was that? Hers, I bet. Quick, in Nell's room, on her bed, while the storm lasts, before we find out, before the cop arrives, hat in hand. We'll do it for her. We'll keep her bed warm. We'll burrow into her sheets, into her body smell. We'll fight back the day, the harsh light, the grave face, the brutal word.

II.

A BELL RANG beside me in the dark. I was lying on the sofa in the cold. It rang five or six times and stopped. The silence seemed strange, then I realized it was quiet outside and the storm was gone. I fell back, unsettled. It meant something, that bell. What did it mean? You had to do something.

The bell rang again. I sat up, trying to see in the dark. You have to answer it, of course. I stood up and the ringing stopped. Karl was talking upstairs. The telephone line's down, I thought. They must have fixed it. Yellow linemen in bucket trucks. They haven't fixed the power yet. I held myself tight. *Nell.* A weight dropped inside me. It was news. I didn't want to hear the words. I wanted to stay right here forever, suspended. Like a soldier with one foot on a land mine.

—Ashe! Karl called from upstairs, shining a flashlight down.

I closed my eyes. It was in the house now, searching for me. It would find me in a moment. It would seem strangely ordinary at first, just one more thing. I'd have to explain it to myself, everything it meant.

—Ashe, come here. Quick! There was excitement in his voice. I ran upstairs.

88

—What is it?

—She wants to talk to you.

He gave me the phone.

—Ashe? It was her voice, small, distorted, like on a transistor radio. My knees buckled and I sat on the stairs.

—Mom?

—Can you pick me up?

—You okay?

—The truck's stuck, she said.

—Where are you?

—Falderberry Road. Two miles east of Highway 28 on Falderberry Road. Can you tell them I don't want to talk? Can you just tell them that? Can you ride in the back with me?

—Of course.

—You understand what I mean?

—Yes.

Outside, the air was still after the storm. The fresh snow was blue in the moonlight. Karl and I scraped the ice off his car windows. He got in and read the instructions to a new set of tire chains.

—They're easy, I said. You just start with the back part.

—Let me get oriented.

He held up a chain, fingering the blue clasp, comparing it with the diagram. I picked up one of the chains and started putting it on a tire.

—She's waiting, I said. I held the flashlight in my teeth and hooked on the back part of the chain first, then the front. *See?* I said.

He wasn't looking.

—Don't worry about it, I said, I'll put them on. Just look at the map. Find out where she is.

He kept reading the instructions.

—It says they're dangerous if they're not put on right, he said.

—They're on right! I always do it. Just look at the map. She's cold.

—Did she say that?

—Yes.

—You didn't say that upstairs.

—What do you think? Her truck broke down. It's cold outside.

He flipped through the map book. Susan came out and sat in the front passenger seat. I finished the chains and got into the back, sitting on my hands to warm them.

—There's no Falderberry road, Karl said.

—What about Alderberry? Susan said.

—Nothing like that. Halderberry, Calderberry, Palderberry. There's nothing.

—Go to Highway 28, I said. We'll look at the crossroads. It'll be there.

—We don't know which way to turn on 28.

—We can ask someone.

—There won't be anyone there at this time.

—Just go! We'll find her, I said, thinking of the gun and her flat voice.

—How are we going to find her? Can you tell me that? Karl said. Why didn't you ask her for directions?

—Just go! You jackass! I shouted, hitting his seat. Just go! For Chrissakes!

Karl turned around.

—What did you call me?

—A jackass. A born fool.

—I've had enough of this, he said, and turned the engine off.

—Just forget it! Susan shouted. Go!

—No. I'm not forgetting it. I'm going to get something straight with this child, once and for all.

—*Ah, ah, ah, ah, ah,* I said, mimicking Susan's moan.

Karl's mouth opened and shut.

—You going now? I said. We have to find her.

Susan's head was shaking. She's laughing, I thought, and I started to smile, but it was sobbing.

—You won't tell her. Ashe! Please. *Please!* she said. It was a mistake. It will kill her!

—She's cold, I said.

—You won't tell her, will you?

—Let's go! I shouted. For fuck's sake!

He started the car and lurched forward. The tires plowed through the snow, the chains biting on the gravel. Ahead, the frozen pool in the ditch was swept clean by the wind rounding the garage. Reeds stood in thick clusters in the milky ice, their white tops like little faces. I thought of her waiting in the truck, her face blank, like the voice on the phone. I recognized the tone. I used it myself when I was very tired. You let the voice talk by itself from the throat.

We drove in the middle of the road through the thick snow, the car swaying from side to side. Karl's high beams didn't work. The low beams lit only a short stretch in front of us. Anything might appear out of the darkness and we wouldn't be able to stop—a deer, a child, Nell herself, kneeling on the road, her arms held out to us. Karl had the windshield wipers on though it wasn't snowing. They clicked and squealed, stroking the dry glass. I knew I'd tell Nell about the two of them, even if I didn't want to, even if I promised not to. It was inevitable. I could feel it inside me, straining to get out.

—This is 28, Karl said. Left or right?

—North, I said.

—North? Susan said, looking at me.

—Pretty sure, I said.

That's where I would go, away from town, away from people. We went north and drove for a long time. It was grey outside, the fields and trees were just visible. I read the road signs over Susan's shoulder.

—Falderberry! I shouted.

—Where? You sure? Karl asked.

—No. I think.

Karl turned the car around. It was Falderberry all right, a narrow farm road, just two tire ruts in the snow. It led up a steep incline. We climbed the hill, skidding and jerking on the chains. At the top Karl stopped the car.

—Look, we have to talk about this, he said.

—Leave the kid alone! Susan shouted. He'll do whatever he wants. Just *go!*

—Goddammit! he said, slamming the car into gear. I could see the outline of Susan's face.

It was such a small thing, I thought. Like stuffing yourself with food. And what did Nell care? She didn't even talk to Karl. And last night, Susan was waiting for the police to knock on our door. I touched her shoulder. She cupped my hand. Her fingers were cold. Guilt, I thought. I didn't want to tell. I felt sorry for her—her heaving grunts, her muffled scream, her moment of joy. It was all ruined now. I won't tell, I won't tell, I thought. But I knew I would, nonetheless.

Nell was standing in the road near a farmhouse. The truck was slumped over in the ditch. We stopped beside her, and she got into the back with her bag. There was a bruise on her forehead.

—Did you hit your head? Karl said. Remember what they said about your concussion.

—Can you take me home? she said.

—Are you all right? he said. Did you bump your head? Let me check your pupils.

—Just take me home, Karl! Please!

Karl missed the clutch, and we shuddered forward. Nell leaned against the door with her eyes closed. After a few minutes she was still. I reached through the curtain of her hair and locked her door. I could smell alcohol on her breath.

—Mom? I said.

She didn't move. Watching her face, I quietly unzipped her bag. It better not be there, I thought. Fucking bitch if she brought it back. At the bottom, under her clothes, was something heavy wrapped in a towel. I unravelled it and felt the gun. I took it out and slipped it into my pocket.

We drove along the white country lane until we came to a paved road, recently cleared of snow, still striated from the snowplows.

—Can we stop here for a minute? I said. I have to pee.

Karl pulled over and Nell flopped forward. She sat up, opened her eyes for a moment, then rested her head against the window. I got out and climbed over the snowbank and up the slope and into the woods. The trees were on the edge of a steep gully. I took out the gun. It was an old revolver, a six-shooter. There were two bullets side by side in the cylinder. She'd been serious, I thought. I imagined some hotel maid finding her on the floor, not knowing who she was, how she rubbed her face when she slept, how she mixed up her words when she woke, how she turned soft when you finally said sorry. You pull the trigger and everything ends. All around me the branches were bare and twisted. One squeeze and you're gone. You were never here, never even born.

I turned the cylinder until a bullet was in the firing position, cocked the gun and raised it in both hands. I could wake her up right now, I thought. Give her a taste . . . I touched the trigger as I adjusted my grip and the gun went off in my hands, knocking me back against a tree, scattering the birds overhead. My ears screamed as I stood up, and all I could think of was I had to initiate, the jolt had opened something inside me. I unzipped and pushed my belly forward and it streamed out of me, the hot liquid eating through the snow, making black yellow-rimmed holes. I zipped up with one hand and caught myself and yelled, dropping the gun in the snow. I bent over and eased the zipper down. There was a bloody track of blue and red teeth marks on the delicate skin. I zipped up carefully and picked up the gun and limped out into the open.

Nell was beside the car staring up at me, her hand over her mouth. Susan and Karl were climbing the bank.

—I've got your gun, I shouted, my ears ringing hard. I raised it to my head in salute.

She fell to her knees. I dropped my arm and walked into the trees, ready to fling the gun down the gulley. But at the edge of the steep slope, I shoved it under my belt against my back and picked up a rock and threw that instead. It clattered through the trees, snapping the dry branches.

When I came out, Karl was shouting at me. I held up my hands. *I threw it,* I shouted, pointing at the woods. He went into the trees to find the gun. Nell was walking toward me, saying something I couldn't make out. Susan had her arm around her as they climbed up the slope. Karl came back from the woods and they were all talking together, and I was staring right at Nell, right into her wet eyes, and I didn't give a damn she was crying. Susan was pulling me by the arm. I twisted and broke away from her. *No, I'm not going with her,* I shouted. *I'm not going with that bitch!*

In the end, Karl took Nell down the hill and drove her home and Susan stayed with me by the trees. She kept talking to me, trying to calm me down. I shook my head as I watched the car disappear down the road. *Go with your boyfriend,* I said. Susan stopped talking and stood beside me and held my hand. I didn't pull away. I turned toward her to hide the bulge against my back. She put her arms around me. The contact made me want to hold her, but I kept my arms down. *I'll never trust her again*, I said. She nodded. Then she was crying and I held her. When she stopped, we stood leaning together with our hands frozen in our pockets waiting for Karl to return. My ears were ringing the whole time, and the gun's kick was buzzing in my neck.

He finally came back and drove us home, and I fell asleep in the car. It was mid-morning when we reached the house. Susan and Karl wanted to talk about what had happened, but I went straight upstairs to my room and locked the door. Even now there was a faint ringing in my ears, an electronic sound that meant the cells were dead and you'd never hear that sound again. It was perfectly steady, like the pain in my chest.

I lay on my bed with the gun. It was an old Italian sidearm from World War II. Dad had brought it back as a souvenir from the war. There was no trigger guard, and the trigger folded back out of the way so it wouldn't snag in your pocket. The barrel was octagonal, and there was a hidden rod for ejecting the bullets. It was hard to load, hard to fire, and hard to unload. But you could turn the cylinder by hand, which meant you could play Russian Roulette. How many soldiers played that game, I wondered, when they couldn't take it anymore? There was only one bullet left, as far as I knew. Nell might have some hidden away.

All the time I was lying there, a question kept forming in my mind, a question she must have asked herself: What's it like afterwards? When everything's quiet. When you're not there to see what's happened. You're folded to a single point. So nothing's there, not even *nothing*, just the meaning of the word itself, fading away, like an echo, like the TV fading to a dot.

I would only have to lift the barrel to my head and rest it on my temple. The last bullet is quiet, I thought. She'd tried to do it herself, but she'd failed. And I knew why she'd failed. You have to work up to it slowly. You can't rush yourself. You hold the empty gun to your head and pull the trigger. You do it over and over again, getting used to the motion, like a soldier drilling for war. Then, when the time is right, you do it without thinking.

I closed my eyes and turned the cylinder around. I thought, One in six. I cocked the hammer and held the barrel to my head. A one-in-six chance. I could do it. Right now, with one squeeze. Up and out. I'll show you how it's done, Mom. I felt for the trigger and pulled it down, locking it into the open position. I rested my finger against it for a moment, then I heaved over, coughing up bile. I flung the gun away. I listened for footsteps outside, but it was quiet. They were all asleep. I lay back, tasting the acid bile, then I rolled off the bed and went over to the gun and knelt beside it. The hammer was still cocked. It would have fired if it had hit the wrong way. I turned the cylinder so the chamber was empty and released the hammer. The gun was so heavy in my hand, a pure weight of balanced steel, a real instrument of war, so many terrible things it had seen. I opened the loading latch, locking the firing hammer, and carefully pried out the bullet, then I polished the gun with a cloth and put it on my pillow and lay down with the barrel under my cheek, the burnt-bullet smell right there beside me.

I had sharp violent dreams all that day. I'd be firing the gun at somebody and I'd wake in a cold sweat and feel for the gun under the covers, making sure the trigger was safely up, then I'd be back in the dream again, racing through flames in the old house, riding on horseback through a battlefield, running through a bombed-out city under fire, trying to save my friend, trying to save my brother, but there wasn't enough time. Then Nell was searching for the gun and I hid from her in a wet dugout, and she walked around the field, kicking the turf as she went, and I stared at her every move, ready to shoot her dead rather than give it up.

I WOKE AT dusk and went downstairs. Karl was sitting in the living room in the dark. He brought Susan and me into the dining room and sat across from us as if we were his clients. In a patient voice he explained why Nell had taken the gun with her. She'd no intention of using it, he said. She just didn't want to leave it lying around in case Ashe found it. She'd tried to get away for a few days to clear her head, that was all. It was perfectly reasonable, if you think about it. She'll be coming out of her room very soon now. *Very* soon.

Susan picked crumbs off the tablecloth as he spoke, then rose and went to the kitchen.

—She's lying, I said to Karl. You do know that, don't you?

He raised his eyebrows, saying nothing.

—You're a fool, I said.

—Sticks and stones, he said quietly.

—What about the truck?

—We'll get it fixed. She'll need it to get around.

—And what did she say about you and Susan screwing on her bed? I said.

He just shook his head and went upstairs.

We'll get it fixed. It was the two of them now, just the way he wanted. I went into the kitchen, where Susan was washing the dishes, though they were already clean. She looked over at me but kept scrubbing.

—She's lying, I said.

She stopped and stared down at the sink. Then she started scrubbing again.

—Look, Ashe, I really don't . . . I just don't know, she said.

—She's lying. You know she's lying. The gun was loaded when I got it. Why'd she put bullets in it if she wanted to keep it away from me?

She kept washing the dishes.

—Anyway, she said, it's over now.

I went upstairs and locked my door and lay on my bed.

A tree branch snaps off in a storm. It's lying there on the ground, waiting to be carted away. They say, *No, no, it's all right. It'll reattach itself.* But it's lying at your feet. It's sheared clean off, the flesh-white wood open to the air. *No, don't worry,* they say, *it's fine. Give it time.*

THAT NIGHT, I went into Will's room and pushed his bed against the wall right next to her bedroom, three feet from where she lay. I put my hands against the wall.

The day of Will's funeral, she'd stopped the truck at the end of the driveway and stared back across the grounds in silence.

What did she see there?

Not some building, some collection of steeples and porticos and windows, but the house itself, the house you saw after living there for many years. It was waiting for her to return, like an old grizzled dog waiting for its owner. It had seen such things before. Many times. *Don't worry*, it was saying, *this will pass. Be consoled.* She shook her head and drove on.

Everything that day said the same thing. The church by the roadside, the faces of the people, the words in the mass, the sun on the ice, the windblown ceremony on the hill. *It will pass. It's happened millions of times before. Look at the bare branches around you. Every fallen leaf is a person gone. Every person had a ceremony. Be consoled.*

I will not, she said. I can feel him inside me. I feel his nails scraping away like a rat in a hog's belly. Nothing else of him is left.

12.

I GOT BACK from school and there was an envelope on my bed. My name was written on the front in big girlie letters. The edges were embossed with flowers like a wedding invitation. Inside was a card with the words:

SATURDAY, 10 A.M., OLD BARN, RSVP.

I flicked it at the wall. Then I went over and ground it under my heel. I picked it up and read it again. *Old Barn.* The card was curved like a cupped hand, the raised flowers were flat and soiled. I won't go. I lay on the bed and closed my eyes. All day I'd wanted to lie down and sleep, but now her note kept playing on my mind. She would have posted it herself, climbing up the hill with the letter in her hand, pursing her lips as she picked her footing in the snow, planting her bad leg, then dipping sideways as she hobbled forward.

I went downstairs to the living room and phoned Sheila's house. Her sister, Cara, answered. She was three years older than Sheila and me, but she treated us like kids.

—That Ashe? Why don't you come by anymore? she said. Don't you like older girls?

—Why would I go over? You're just a tease.

—Ashe, boy! Don't say that. Come on *by*. You must. I want to see you. I won't tease. I promise.

—When have you ever kept a promise?

—Don't be an old man. Are you coming to see me or not?

—You still single?

—I might be. Why'd you ask? Are you interested? You know I'm yours, don't you, Ashley? You just have to ask. It's the sailor, she said to Sheila.

—You back with Simon?

—No. Come on by. I'll tell you about our big fight. I'll tell you what he said to me. I can't say it on the phone. Here she is.

Cara gave the phone to Sheila.

—You're supposed to mail an answer back, Sheila said. Seriously, I want to get at least one letter before I'm an old spinster.

—What are you doing now? I said.

—I'm busy.

—Let's go now.

—No, I'm busy. Can't you wait to see me? I could hear her smiling.

—So what is it? You found something? I said.

—I may have.

—Are you going to show me or what?

—Maybe. You've got to say you want to see me, though. You have to say it.

—Let's just wait then.

—I don't mind. I already know what it is.

—All right, all right. I want to see it.

—No, say you want to see *me—me!* You have to say it, she said.

—I—want—to—see—you. Okay? Jesus.

—Then hurry up, boy. Use your bike.

The street was narrow because of the snowbanks. I rode along the tire troughs where the snow was compressed. I pedalled fast for two miles, crouching low like a racer, watching over my shoulder for cars, then turned off at Sheila's farm and leaned my bike against the fence and walked across the snow to the old barn. Inside, it was dark except for the thin light shining through the walls. I could see the sky and the outline of trees between the boards. The barn was on its last legs. Some storm would blow it over soon. It had been empty for years but it still smelled of live animals—dung and urine and feed. There were stalls along both walls and an office at the back, up a log staircase. I saw Sheila in the office window looking down at me, her head resting on her palms. I opened my arms wide to her, but she didn't move. I took off my coat and flung it on the ground and unbuttoned my jeans and turned around and let them slide down my legs, showing her my bare ass. A gust of wind hit me up the back, and I crouched over and pulled my pants up and ran up the stairs.

—Was that for me? she said.

—Of course.

—*Lucky* me.

The room was ten feet square with two windows, one looking

out over the field and one looking in over the barn. In the middle of the room was a wooden table with four chairs, and along one wall was a bench. There was a space heater on the ground blowing hot air. I took off my jacket.

—There's power in here? I said.

—Mike and Josh hooked it up. They play poker here.

I sat down on a chair, and she stood over me with her arms crossed.

—So? she said. How is she?

—The same. Still in her room.

—Does she talk to you now?

—No. She just stays there.

She touched my cheek, then she bent down and kissed me on my lips, the merest touch, which skated over my neck and arms and back. I took her hand and pulled her over to the bench and sat beside her.

—Can I? I said.

She nodded and tilted her head back so I could kiss her, but I touched her face instead. She stiffened as I traced under her eyes, along her nose, across her cheek, down her neck. She trembled when I stroked her shoulder and pulled away.

—Let's lie down, she whispered. I remembered the thunderstorm and her wet eyes looking up at me. She dragged out a green rucksack from under the bench.

—Sometimes they sleep here after poker, she said. She pulled out a foam mattress and two sleeping bags. We arranged them on the floor and lay down. She rested her head in the crook of my arm.

—You're beautiful, I said. Do you know that?

—What about my leg?

—That's your best part. You'd be one of those pretty-pretty girls otherwise.

I stroked her bad leg through her jeans. She pushed my hand away.

—I *hate* my leg, she said. I can't stop thinking about it.

—You'd be like Cara, always trying to catch someone looking at you.

—No I wouldn't. I hate people looking at me.

—Let me see it, I said, squeezing her leg.

—What? No!

—I want to see it, come on.

—No! she said. Why do you want to see it?

—How many boys have seen it?

—None. Not even my brothers.

—That's why, I said. Just let me see it once.

—No, I'd have to take my pants off.

—I don't mind. I'll take mine off if you want.

—You will not! She pushed me away.

—Come on. Let me see it.

—It's awful.

—Please.

To my surprise, she stood up.

—Turn around, she said.

I looked out the window at the farm. Half the trees had branches pointing down and half had branches pointing up, as if some had blown inside out in the wind like umbrellas. Why was she showing me? She wants to, I thought. She wants to. I liked the sound of the words. She wants to. My heart was thumping.

—Okay, she said. She was standing with the sleeping bag in front of her. Her jeans were folded on the bench.

—I won't show you the whole leg, she said, talking from her throat like she might cry.

—Look, you don't have to show me. It's okay, I said, my face hot.

She dropped the sleeping bag and there it was, an old man's leg. Her good leg was curved and muscular with dimples in the thigh; the old man's leg was bony and mottled with white papery skin. The kneecap was flat, with wrinkles across it, like a loose sock. I reached forward and felt the skin. It was dry and smooth. A birch tree.

—Does it hurt?

—It aches sometimes. Her voice was gentle.

Her real voice, I thought. It surprised me more than the leg. She spoke to herself with that voice. I looked up at her, and she looked away.

—Thank you, I said.

She stood over me, holding my head against her soft belly, trembling slightly.

—Come on, lie down, I said. She wiped her face, and we lay together.

—Does that hurt? she said in the same gentle voice, pointing at my raised crotch.

—No. It will go down.

She put her hand between my legs and rubbed up and down. I winced with the pain.

—What's wrong? she said.

—Nothing. I've got a cut, that's all. The scabs have just opened.

—You cut yourself?

—With my zipper.

—My God, I thought it was me. I thought I hurt you.

She reached up and held my cheeks.

—Don't be shy with me, little boy. I'm a farm girl, you know.

I stretched over and touched her breasts, but she pushed my hand away.

—No.

—Why not?

—I don't like it.

She sat up and held her arms over her chest.

—I don't want you to.

—You're a tease.

—I'm not. I'm *not*. Don't say that. I just don't like being . . . touched.

—Why not?

—I don't know. I hate it. I've always hated it. I thought it would go away, but it won't.

She turned her back on me, holding her legs with her arms.

—You don't like to be touched? Is that all? It's all right. I don't care.

—You don't mind?

—No . . . it's nothing.

—I'm sorry. It's not you. I just hate being touched. I feel like I'm suffocating.

—It's nothing. Really.

—I know it's weird. That's why I never go near boys.

—Look, it's just me here. No one else has to know.

—You don't care?

—Sheila, I don't mind really. It's fine with me.

She nodded, wiping the tears away.

—You all right? I said.

—Yes.

—It's not like I didn't already know.

—I'm sorry.

—It's okay. Maybe you can touch me . . . sometime. When you're ready. If you want to. I won't touch you back.

She nodded.

—Really?

—Maybe . . . later, she said.

She lay beside me again and pulled my arm around her.

—You can hug me lightly. That's all right.

We stared at the ceiling, the whirring heater tripping on and off.

—I *will*, she said quietly. When I'm . . . ready.

—Remember the storm? I said.

—Yes. I wanted to go swimming . . .

—You were scared of the thunder.

—I hate that noise. She made a thunder sound in her throat.

—You were shaking all over.

—You held me gently. You were lovely.

—You asked me to hold you, I said. You made me.

—It was like in a movie.

—You were shaking like mad. There's a dog next door that shakes like that. Sergeant Monte. You put a leash on him and he shakes just like that.

—We should have gone swimming, she said.

—We couldn't. It was a storm.

—It was just rain. I was crazy that night. I would have shown you my leg, and everything else. *Everything*. And I'd hidden beers for us. We could have gone skinny-dipping.

—Why didn't we? I said.

—You didn't want to, remember? And then we fell asleep.

—Will would have killed me. Can you imagine? I got drunk with a girl and went skinny-dipping. Sorry you missed it.

—What'd he say about us sleeping together? she said.

—I didn't tell him. He felt bad enough as it was, missing the party.

—I've something to show you, she said, getting up and looking through her jacket. I saw a flash of white panties under her blouse. It made her skin look yellow. She held up an envelope.

—Your uncle's? I said.

—My great-uncle's. I found it in one of the boxes.

Her great-uncle had died a few weeks before, and she'd helped clear his house so they could sell the property. They had boxes of his things in their basement.

—Here. She held out the handwritten letter to me.

—You read it, I said.

She sat back on the bench, resting her feet on the edge of the seat, forgetting about her bad leg. The white cloth of her panties was dark between her thighs, the hair crushed under the fabric, like hay stuffed in burlap, a few strands poking through the weave. It was fascinating to the eye. I wanted to stroke it with my finger. I stared at her face as she read, trying not to look down but glancing now and then.

—*Dear R*—that's for Richard, dear Richard—*I saw your wife yesterday. A sour old puss she had on her. She looks right miserable. What did you do to her? She didn't start off that way, I'm guessing. She was quite beautiful once, I've been told. Didn't she get enough? Or did she get too much? Is that it? Did you plough her night and day until she was no use to anyone? I wonder. A farmer and his field. And what about me? What do you have in store for me?*

—It doesn't say that, I said.

—I swear. *Look.* She held it out, and I could see *plough her night and day* over her thumb.

—Who's it from?

—Let me read it first. It's from his mistress. *What do you have in store for me? I wouldn't mind, anyway. It would be nice to be used up. But where have you been? I heard all about Tuesday. You were drinking with the boys again, weren't you? And don't bother denying it. I have my sources. Why didn't you come over? Are you tired of me already? You keep wasting time. How long do you think we have? I keep asking myself that.*

How long do we have? I was in the garden the whole day waiting for you. Then to find you were boozing with Clyde, of all people—surely you can understand my surprise. Nora just blurted it out right there in the street. I nearly slapped her in front of everyone. I'm pestering you, aren't I? I don't mean to, believe me. Go have your fun if you must. How I hate the flowers this year. How garish they are. But they do smell nice. I've been thinking about you all day. I've been so angry, but I keep thinking about you. I can't stop myself. I picked some rose petals and went behind a tree and rubbed them all over. All over. Even there—that lonely place you once took such an interest in.

—What? She rubbed them where? You mean down there?

—Wait. Just listen. *That lonely place you once took such an interest in. I'm afraid she won't forgive you this time. You know what she's like. Perhaps if you made amends. I'm sure if you washed her she'd forgive you. Shall we call that your punishment? Now, listen to this. You must kneel before her and wash her like a cat. It's the only way, I'm afraid.* It's signed O. And then at the bottom it says, *I'm tired of it. I'm tired of missing you and all of it. I can't sleep anymore. Don't touch her, please. Please! You promised me. You know I can't bear it.*

Sheila looked at me triumphantly.

—It's sad at the end, I said. Who is she?

—It says on the envelope, look. He wrote it in pencil. Olivia Granger.

—Who's that?

—Some farmer's wife. She lived next door to him. She's dead now.

—But the two of them, carrying on like that, behind everyone's back. It's amazing. *Amazing!*

She was pleased and lay down again.

The room was hot, but the heater was on the other side of the room and I didn't want to get up.

—They never tried to marry or anything? I said.

—No. They were just lovers.

—Imagine. Licking her like a cat.

—Tell me a story, she said. Tell me about the girl in the storm.

—Come on. Not again.

—Tell me, tell me. Don't be like that.

—Christ, I said. Once upon a time I went to a party.

—No, from the beginning, and tell it properly, not in that voice.

—Okay, okay. Cara was helping my mom in the garden, and she asked me to come to her party.

—But why did she ask you? Remember? Because you were sad.

—All right then, I was sad.

—And why were you sad?

—I can't remember. Something.

—Where was Will?

—I don't know. Look, I'm not telling it if you keep asking questions.

—I won't. Go on. I won't say a word.

—We were late for the party because the car broke down and we had to phone Rob Stiller to come out and fix it, and when we finally got there, everyone was going in and out of the cabin, and Cara was really pissed off because someone had jimmied open the door instead of waiting for her, and she found out it was that Fred asshole who'd done it, and he was just lying there on a deck chair grinning up at her, so she got a bucket of swamp water and dumped it over his head. And then they started a campfire and we all cooked hot dogs.

Sheila sat up and crossed her legs. I caught a faint piquant smell with the motion.

—What happened then, exactly? she said, looking down at me. Tell me exactly what happened.

—I was just sitting there, and I saw this girl talking to these older girls.

—What did she look like?

—She looked like a little china doll, I said, with black hair cut straight across her eyebrows. Like Cleopatra.

—Was she pretty?

—No. She was ugly, like Cleopatra. And she pretended she didn't see me, even though Cara told her to say hello. But she was too cool to say hello.

—No she wasn't, she said. What was she wearing?

—A long summer dress right down to her shoes.

—Did she walk funny?

—She limped a little, I said. I thought, She'd sprained her ankle or something.

—So what happened?

—She picked up the little dog that was running around and rubbed it all over her face, so I thought, She's probably not that bad, not like some pretty girls. But she still wouldn't look at me.

—They were playing baseball, she said.

—Yeah, these two drunk guys were playing catch, and they were throwing it really hard without gloves. You could hear it smacking into their hands, and they were getting angry at each other, and then I looked around and the girl was sitting right behind me, and she said, *They're going to fight, just wait.* And then they started fighting, just like she said, but they kept falling down in the mud, they were so drunk. And after a while they started laughing and slapping each other on the back. And then we walked around together, and we saw Cara's boyfriend.

—Ian. I remember him. I liked him, she said. Tell me about Ian.

—He was standing by himself and he opened a can of beer they'd shaken up, and it sprayed all over him, but he just laughed. And then Cara came over and she was being all shy—or she was pretending to be shy—and she held me in front of her and talked to him over my head. And then it started raining, and we all ran into the house.

—You had your arm around me, she said. You were worried about me, weren't you?

—It was thundering like mad and you were shaking all over, and the house was full of all these drunk guys, shouting and laughing. So we went into a bedroom and locked the door.

—And then? she said. What did we do in the bedroom?

—You held me and said, *Do you like me?* and I said yes. And then you asked me again, and I said yes. And it was thundering really loud, and you were shivering like crazy, and you kept asking me if I liked you, and I kept saying, *Yes, I like you, yes.* And then the lightning flashed really bright, and you were crying.

—You were nice, she said, and she turned and kissed me, and her breath went into my mouth.

—What happened then? she said.

—You asked me if I'd lie down with you, so we lay down on the bed, and you fell asleep. And then they started blaring this music outside, and I was sure you were going to wake up, but you didn't. And there was this big crowd dancing on the lawn, and they were all wet and muddy, and they had their arms up in the rain, and they had lined up all these cars so the headlights were shining across the field. And they were playing that song "Dirty Woman," over and over.

—How does it go?

—*Dirrr-ty woman, dirrr-ty woman,* I sang. *She loves her preacher man. She grinds him in the nighttime, she grinds him in the day, she grinds him in the chapel—*

She put her finger over my lips.

—*She grinds the dirt away,* she sang.

—Then *Dirty woman, dirty woman* over and over. It goes on forever.

—*She grinds the dirt away,* she said again, smiling at me.

—Then Cara woke us up and said we should have waited until the wedding, and she drove us home.

—Did you look at me when I was sleeping?

—No, it was dark.

—You didn't look at my leg?

—No.

—You weren't even curious about it?

—I didn't think about it.

—You're lying. You looked at it.

—It's always about your stupid leg, isn't it?

—I hate my leg, she said. I don't care what anyone says.

She stared out the window.

—Did you ever see a white fox? I said. An albino?

—No.

—I saw one once. It was pure white, just like snow. It looked like an Arctic fox or something. They're so rare. I didn't even know they could survive in the wild. I kept going back to where I'd seen it, but I couldn't find it again ... You never remember a red fox, Sheila. You see them all the time, but you don't remember them, do you? Then one day, you see a white fox, and you never forget it.

She looked at me.

—A white fox ... she said quietly. Ashe, you know that night at Cara's party? You know why I spoke to you? I saw you sitting there by yourself, and I thought, What's up with this one? Why does he look that way? So quiet, so ... distant.

She leaned down and put her forehead against mine.

—Turn your head while I dress, she said.

I turned and watched the coiled orange glow in the heater, bright in the fading light.

—Why doesn't your mother like me? she said as she dressed.

—It's not you. I mean, it's not *just* you. She doesn't like anyone, I don't think.

—She scares me. Remember when I gave her the flower?

—She's not like that. Not really. She's fed up right now. She's had enough.

—Enough of what?

—Of everything.

13.

No ONE COULD stop her leaving again. She didn't have her truck yet, but she could go on foot any time she wanted to. She only had to walk to the highway and hitch a ride to town or wait and catch a bus. She didn't have to leave at all; there were endless ways to make an exit. Her bathroom cabinet was full of prescription medicines, and there were poisons and chemicals everywhere in the house, rat poison and cleaners and solvents and other things, and there were knives and razors and—of course—rope. There were so many places to string up a rope. If you fell from high enough you'd snap your neck clean and feel nothing. Like putting a bullet in your head. Just go up to the second floor in the old house and tie a rope to the joist and jump into the ballroom. That's how I would do it. Get good and drunk and stand on the banisters and fall. Then you're not hanging there, choking to death. So many places, so many ways. Give her long enough, she'd figure it out. She was thinking it through, the easiest and hardest of all problems, how to trick the terrified body to do what it's told and turn on itself.

~~~~~~~~~

I HEARD KARL's car leaving, and I went down to the kitchen. Susan was peeling potatoes.

—When are they finished with the truck? I said. When will it be ready?

—I don't know.

—Is he giving it back to her?

—Ashe, it's her truck, we can't keep it from her.

—Why not? Of *course* you can keep it from her. Don't give her the keys, that's all. What'll she do about it? Just give them back when she's better.

—We can't do that. It's not ours.

—Don't be so stupid. She'll take off again if you give it to her.

—Ashe, she's mending. She's getting better. She spoke to Karl today.

—That's because she wants the truck back. That's the only reason she spoke to him.

—Ashe.

—No, you're as dumb as he is. Look, if he gives her the truck, I'll wreck it for him, tell him that. I'll wreck it for good. And he better hide his own car keys. She stole them last time. If he leaves them lying about. I'll drive his car away. He can call his cop friends on me.

—Calm down, would you? What's got into you anyway? Why are you saying all this?

—You're *useless*, Susan. Just useless.

I went to my room and packed a knapsack with clothes and the gun, and I carried it down with Will's winter sleeping bag.

—I'm not eating, I said.

—God, Ashe, everything's a big drama with you. We're trying our best here. Why aren't you eating, tell me that. I've been slaving away for you.

I grabbed a loaf of bread from the cupboard and a block of cheese from the fridge and put them in a paper bag and filled a bottle with water.

—What's that for? she said.

—I'm leaving.

—No you're not. Just *stop* it, would you. Where are you going?

I pointed out the window to the shed.

—Over there. I'm not staying here anymore.

She reached out to me, and I stepped back.

—See you, Aunt Susan.

—You're leaving me here by myself?

I shoved the food and the rolled-up sleeping bag into the knapsack.

—Tell Karl, if he brings the truck back, I'll wreck it. Just tell him that for me.

I carried the knapsack and the water across to the shed.

LYING IN THE shed in the sleeping bag with a tennis racquet in my hand, I waited for Karl to come, watching my breath with the flashlight, the beam fading slowly to orange as the batteries died. I was certain he'd come. I listened for the crunch of the snow, playing the scene through in my mind. Karl shouts, *Enough of this. Enough! You can't threaten us, boy. Get back into the house!* He tries to pull me out of the shed, and I hit him on the head with the racquet. I bit down on my lip thinking how I'd hit him—hard enough that he'd strike back and then I'd yell and Nell would come to the window.

LONG AFTER DARK, the wind picked up and blew a hollow tone through the vents in the roof. A dog howled in the distance. There was no lock on the door. I found a broom and pushed it against the door and rested the other end on my leg. At least I'd feel the door open.

The lights in Nell's bedroom turned on, and her hair flashed in the window. She was going to the washroom. A minute later she was back, and the lights went off and she stood at the window. I shone the flashlight on my face so she'd see me there. I stayed that way for a minute, watching the shapes in the silver reflector, feeling an animal discomfort of blindness and exposure in the dark. *I'm watching you now. I'm watching you.* I turned the flashlight off, and by the time the orange glow had died away, she was gone.

That night, I dreamt of burning the house down. I poured a clear liquid into two jugs from a metal can and watered the flowers in the house and they grew into a jungle, then the liquid smelled like turpentine, and I doused everything and lit the place ablaze, and I became the flame itself, rolling through the rooms and sweeping up the stairs like a boy with a cape. I dissolved the house and everything in it—Karl and Susan and Nell. I felt them disappear like handfuls of snow under a tap. Everyone was happy, including the house, the thing I cared most about because it was so old and sad and couldn't speak for itself. I held the pieces of the house against my groin and released them with the liquid flames. They floated away in a stream of silver smoke. It was pleasant, like drying clothes in the sun so they feel warm and clean when you put them on in the evening.

14.

AFTER A GRUELLING day at school, I walked home from the school bus and found there was a new lock on the garage door and heavy bars over the windows. Inside was Nell's truck, good as new, washed and ready to go. Busy Karl, I thought. Doing his duty, following orders.

I went straight to the shed and got into the sleeping bag with my clothes on. I could try forcing the slats under the garage roof and squeezing in. But even if I got in and wrecked the truck, Karl would just have it fixed again and put up new bars.

I ROSE IN the night, wrapped the gun in a towel and took it outside into the woods. I climbed up a tree and hid the gun in a crevice and then walked over to the kitchen. The lights were off, which meant Karl and Susan were asleep. I ate cold pasta from the fridge and sat in the living room. Just after one o'clock, the hall light turned on and Nell came downstairs and went to the kitchen. I leaned my ear against the kitchen door and listened to her moving about inside, then I pushed the door open quietly. She was in an old track suit, eating pasta with her fingers in front of the open fridge. She had patches of red skin around her nose and on her forehead, and her hair was a mess. She turned around and saw me.

—*Jesus!* she shouted. Jesus Christ. You scared me!

She put the bowl back in the fridge and wiped her mouth.

—What are you doing there? She turned her back on me and fixed her hair.

—I'm looking at you, aren't I?

—I'm a sight, don't look.

She turned the stove light on and switched off the kitchen light and stood against the fridge with her arms crossed.

—Is that breakfast or dinner? I said.

—I don't know. Both. I'm hungry is all. You scared the hell out of me.

—I wanted to see you.

—I'm a mess.

—I can see that.

She was shivering like she was standing outside.

—Look, Ashe, give me some time.

—I'm not Karl, I said. You don't have to use that voice. You don't have to pretend.

—Whatever it is, I can't. Not right now. I'm sorry. I just can't.

—There were two bullets in the gun, I said.

She looked out the window.

—It's hard to load that gun. You opened it and put those bullets there.

—I did, she said.

—You tried to ... You wanted to ... with that gun. Isn't that true?

She held her hands out and dropped them.

—No, she said. It's not true.

—Where did you go then? Where did you take the gun?

—I went to get drunk, if you must know, good and drunk. I just wanted it with me.

—A *loaded* gun? You needed a loaded gun with you? Sure. I really believe that. Now you got Karl to give you the truck back. Congratulations.

—Ashe, I'm not going anywhere. I tried that and it didn't help.

—No. You're can't say that. You don't know what you're *going* to do. Nobody knows what they'll do tomorrow, or someday. You worked on Karl and got your truck back, and it's right outside, all safe for you.

—Let me get through this in my own way, Ashe. Leave it alone. Just leave it alone. That's my advice to you. Give me space. I'm not going anywhere in the truck.

—You've already gone somewhere, Mom. We had to pick you up in the middle of the night, remember? You drove the truck drunk right into a ditch. Don't give me your lies, Mom. I'm not Karl.

I waited for her to argue back, but she was quiet.

—I'm here to tell you something, I said. I still have the gun.

—*What?* You've got it?

—Yes. I didn't throw it away. I just told them that. I put it right here in my belt. They never checked. I took it back with me and hid it someplace you'll never find. And if you do anything, I'm going to use it on myself, I swear to God. I will use it. I'm not afraid.

She stared at me for a long time.

—You're going to use it on yourself? she said slowly. Is that what you're saying? You're going to *shoot* yourself?

—I will. I'm not afraid.

—Okay then. Go ahead. Use it now. Don't wait for me. Use it, so I can bury you beside Will and be done with it.

—I'm not going to use it now.

—No, Ashe, go ahead. Get it over with. Use it right now, this very night. I won't stop you.

—Mom ...

—You think it works like that, do you? You think you can make yourself do it because you've threatened someone you will? Tell me one thing, will you wait for my funeral first? Will you see me buried, or will you do it before the funeral so we can be buried together? Tell me. Will you have one last meal or will you do it right away? I really want to know, so I can understand. What's your plan, Ashe?

—I don't have a plan.

—No, I didn't think so. Let's just say, for argument's sake, I call your bluff and I'm gone. What then? You're going to put that gun to your head and pull the trigger, is that right? For what reason? To prove your threat was genuine? But I won't be there to see you do it, will I? You'll only be proving it to yourself. It sounds pretty pointless, doesn't it?

—I don't care what you say, I'm not giving the gun back.

—That's fine. Keep it. I won't make a fuss. But I want you to do one thing for me, I want you to promise you won't touch that gun while I'm alive. You owe me that much. If I'm gone, you can do what you want.

—Mom.

—All right? It's a simple promise. If I'm alive, you won't play with the gun. You won't touch it. Just promise me that.

—Okay, I promise.

—The day I'm gone, you can do whatever you want.

—You're such a bitch.

—I'm not a nice person, Ashe. It's true. I know that. And I wish I cared about it, but I don't seem to right now, I'm sorry. I don't know how I'm meant to act these days. Susan told me she slept with Karl, and you found out about it. But the thing I couldn't figure out was why she woke me up to tell me. Does she really think I care what she does with Karl? Because I don't. I really don't care what anyone does. It's not a nice thing. I know that . . . Look, I'm going back upstairs now, but I expect you to keep your promise. I wouldn't expect it from anyone else, but I do from you. I hold you to a higher standard, Ashe.

—I'm not going to touch the gun, I said.

—Okay then.

She walked past me and paused at the door.

—You're the only person I trust, Ashe . . . You're your own man, I know that . . . Everyone else is just wandering around, spinning in the wind, but not you . . . Don't think I haven't noticed.

She went upstairs. Suddenly I was dog-tired. I didn't want to go outside and sleep in the cold. I went into the living room and lay down on the sofa.

15.

IT WAS NIGHT and steaming hot. Spring had brought with it an early heat wave. The shed door was wide open, but there was no breeze. I was soaked with sweat, lying in my shorts on the bare bench. My whole body ached like I'd been digging in a field. Maybe I'd go into the house to sleep. But it would be just as hot inside, and sooner or later it would rain. You could feel it coming. I was thinking of Sheila. Or I was dreaming of her—dreaming then waking, thinking of her. The rain started drumming loudly on the roof. I put my shoes on and went out into the pouring rain and walked around in the dark, letting the water wash over me. I saw something lying in the grass by the trees. I bent down and it was the long wooden ladder the workmen used to fix the roof. I picked it up and carried it to the house and leaned it against Nell's window. I climbed up the ladder and put my face against the wet glass. The room was pitch-black; I could just make out her bed in the corner. I knocked on the window, watching for movement. I kept knocking until her shadow rose from the bed. I waved her over and she came to the window and pulled it up a few inches. She knelt down across from me.

—Come outside. It's *nice*, I said. Come on out. I reached in and pulled her hand. She rested her head on the windowsill.

—Why don't you come out? Come on. It's raining. No one will know.

She didn't move.

—Won't you come out?

—Oh *please*, Ashe. Please.

—Don't you want to come out? It's warm, it's nice.

—Please . . . I do want to. I do.

—Come on then. Just open the window and climb out.

—I can't, she said.

—Look, I've got something for you. Just wait here. Don't close the window. I'll be right back.

I rushed down the ladder and ran across the field into the woods. I climbed up the tall oak tree and got the gun from a cleft in the trunk and climbed down. I ran behind the shed and put the gun on a concrete block, picked up a boulder, and slammed it hard on the barrel. I kept slamming the boulder down until the barrel was crushed, then I ran back to the ladder. She was still sitting there, waiting for me.

—Here, you have it, I said, giving her the gun. I wasn't going to use it. I was just angry. I was never going to use it.

—Thank you, she said.

—Will you come out now?

—Later . . . I'll come out later. I will.

—When will you come out?

—In the summertime.

—No, you have to come out now. You'll never come out later.

—I promise, in the summertime. I will.

—You always want more time.

—I'm sorry . . . I'm tired.

—When will you come out? When?

—When the apples are ripe.

—No. That's not for months.

—It won't be that long.

—It isn't till the end of summer, Mom, it's months away. It has to be sooner. I'll grow some flowers for you, how about that? Right over there, where you can see them. And when they blossom, you'll come out and pick them, all right?

—Maybe.

—You promise you'll pick them?

She didn't say anything.

—You promise? When they blossom, you'll come out. It will be all right. You'll have some more time, then you'll just come down and pick them. I won't tell anyone. You can go back right away. All right?

She nodded.

—You will come out then, when they bloom?

She nodded again.

—Just say you promise.

—I promise. I will.

—Okay then, I'll grow flowers for you, and then you'll come out. That's a promise.

I touched her face but she didn't move.

—I need the keys to the garage. I can't get at the tools.

—Wait, she said.

She went to her table and brought the keys back and handed them to me.

—The frost is over now, I said. I can plant them tomorrow.

She got up and closed the window. I climbed down the ladder and laid it on the ground and went back to the shed. The rain suddenly stopped. I lay on the bench. In the silence, I could hear her voice: *I promise. I will. I promise. I will.*

THE NEXT DAY was Saturday, and as if on cue, Karl left for the weekend, and Susan went into town. I ran over to the garage and unlocked the door and got the weed trimmer down and slopped in some gasoline from a can, wetting my shoes and the floor in my hurry. A few flowers was all. I could grow them with my eyes closed. I pushed some cotton into my ears and, in the seashell hum, I carried the trimmer into the tall grass of the meadow and pumped the engine primer and pulled the cord a few times. It growled and spluttered. I kept pumping the primer until I felt it pick up the fuel, then I gave the cord three quick pulls, and it started with a roar. I squeezed the throttle and revved the engine, the drilling whine rising and falling over a liquid rumble—that nagging summer sound of chainsaws and outboard motors and dirt bikes. I glanced up at the window, but she wasn't there. I pumped the throttle to wake her, racing the engine until it smoked, then I cut the grass in long sweeps.

The trimmer was heavy, and the grass bent in the breeze from the spinning gut, so you had to swing the head back and forth three or four times to cut it properly. I kept squeezing the throttle, racing it like a motorbike. If you attacked the grass at the right speed, you could cut it cleanly with two passes, back and forth. After a couple of hours, I'd cleared an area twenty feet square. I carried the trimmer back to the garage and got a rake and some plastic bags and raked the long grass into piles.

My arms and back ached, and I pulled over a chair and sat on the stubble. I would have to get the power tiller out. You couldn't dig the ground by hand. It was rock hard in the meadow, as if still frozen. Last winter, they'd used a backhoe for Will's grave. You could see the track marks on the hill. They didn't bother peeling off the sod, they just dug it all up, and in the spring they put down new grass. That's how you make a winter grave. The farmers dug the earth every year, the very same earth. And out of that earth came the crops and grass and flowers and trees, all growing in the same soil where you put your brother and your father in solemn ceremonies, where you're thankful for the simple trees and grass.

Ripples raced across the meadow, braking around the bald patch like waves around a rock. I looked at the sun with my eyes closed. I could make the yellow spot turn red by flicking my eyes back into my head. Yellow, red, yellow, red. It felt safe in the heat. They used to worship the sun. You can understand that. It made you feel happy, the sun in your face. Yes, it always said. Yes, yes, yes. That one word.

The tiller had huge propeller blades for churning up the soil.

I filled it with gas and rolled it out from the garage and pushed it over to the field and staked out the flower bed and yanked the starter cord; it ticked over a few times, then roared and chugged like a jackhammer. No one could sleep through that racket. She was wide awake now, listening to me churn up the field. Her field. You promised, I thought. I *made* you promise. You can't back out now. I staggered behind the heavy tiller as it dug into the ground, wobbling forward in a cloud of exhaust. After going over it a few times, I picked out the roots and bulbs; then I plowed it again and picked out more roots and bulbs and pushed the tiller back to the garage. I dragged over a bag of compost and mixed it into the soil.

WHEN SUSAN CAME back from town, I told her that Nell had given me the keys to the garage so I could grow something in the field. She left her bags on the kitchen porch and walked over to the flower bed. She asked me when I had spoken to Nell, but I wouldn't say. I hooked up the hose to the garden faucet and she watched me water the soil until it was drenched. Then she went inside and brought out some chicken curry in a big salad bowl and we ate it in the sun with silver soup spoons. Her mouth had yellow stains at the corners. She quizzed me again about Nell, but I wouldn't tell her.

—Keep your damned secret, she said, but she wasn't really mad.

We sat together listening to the birds. They would clamour over one another and go suddenly quiet, then slowly start up again, first the small birds, then the larger ones.

—I'm planting zinnias, I said. They grow *fast*.

16.

I PLANTED THE seeds and they sprouted in a few days. There was nothing to do but wait for them to grow. I'd lie in the shed listening to the birds, how there were no gaps in the sound, just one long steady stream. You'd have to fire a gun to shut them up, and even then they'd come rushing back at you. I kept thinking of Sheila. I was in a fever over her. I'd strip off in the woods and lie on the ground and touch myself as if I couldn't move and she was exploring me with her strong, uncertain, farm girl fingers. I phoned her up, but she never returned my call. I talked to her sister, Cara, and she promised to make her come over. Finally, one Sunday, she rode over on her bicycle with her hair pulled back, wearing cowboy boots and scruffy jeans and a loose denim shirt—her farm gear. She leaned her bike against the kitchen wall and limped across the field. I took her over to the flower bed. You couldn't see any colour yet, the flower heads were tight green buds.

—What do you think? I said.

—You did this?

—Yes ma'am. I'm a farmer now. It's my first crop.

—Is it for your mother? she said.

—No, it's for someone else.

—For who then?

I tried to kiss her, but she pulled away.

—Don't, she said.

—*Don't.*

—Well.

—*Well.*

She moved away from me and put her hands in her pockets.

—All right, I said. I won't go near you.

—What are they anyway?

—Zinnias.

—What colour?

—I don't know. I don't care about the colour. This or that. I'm growing them is all.

—They look lonesome out here.

—When they're ready, you know what we'll do with them? I said.

—What?

—You know. Can't you think? Can't you remember?

I started rubbing myself up and down.

—*Everywhere* . . . That's what she said, wasn't it? I was looking straight into her eyes. She looked away. There was a crease beside her eye where someday there'd be crow's feet, and the merest hint of down above her lip.

—You didn't phone me back, I said.

—I was busy. I forgot.

—You're such a liar. Why didn't you phone?

—Leave me alone, would you?

—No. I'm not leaving you alone. You don't have to phone me if you don't want. You don't have to do anything. God, it's hot.

I took off my T-shirt and held my arms out wide.

—You're skinny, she said, poking me in the ribs. And pale.

—Don't, I said, moving away from her.

—What's wrong?

—You really have to say it that way? *Leave me alone.*

—I didn't say it like that.

—It's all a person ever hears these days, leave me alone, leave me alone. You won't even phone a guy back.

—What do you want from me, Ashe? Look, I don't know what I said to you in the barn. I didn't mean it, whatever it was. You can't hold me to that.

—I'm not holding you to anything. *Jesus.* I'm not some lawyer, you know. I thought it would be . . . nice . . . I don't know . . . fun. Something.

—Who are the flowers for, really? she said.

—They're for me. For rubbing purposes, I said.

—You're crazy.

—I'm pale and skinny and crazy. Thanks very much.

I put my T-shirt on and started pulling weeds from the soil.

—Is that your aunt? she said, looking over at Susan through the kitchen window.

—Yeah.

—She's still here then?

—As you can see. She's still here.

—Where's your mom?

—She's up there, all right? I pointed at her window. She's right up there. All the time.

—What's she doing?

—She's sleeping, isn't she. She's always sleeping.

—Is that why you're growing these flowers?

—No. I told you why.

—*Hey.*

—What?

—I don't mind that you're pale and skinny.

—Yeah?

I kept weeding. The flowers were scrawny, pitiful things, just stalks and leaves.

—I like flowers, I said, fingering the tiny leaves. They don't mind if you touch them. You can touch them all day long. Doesn't bother 'em at all. Imagine that.

She gave me a stony look.

—Who's the new boyfriend anyway? I said.

—There isn't one, she said. I told you I don't go near boys.

—I noticed.

—Yeah? Well, you can't have a *new* boyfriend if you've never had an old boyfriend, can you? And I've never had any sort of boy-friend my whole life.

—That right?

Her eyes were narrow.

—Do you know someone I will never go with? *Never.* Even if they're the last person alive?

I CARRIED YOU HOME

That stare. Like Nell's. My heart was thumping. I looked down to pull the weeds, not wanting to hear.

—You know who? she said.

—Go ahead then. Tell me.

—A frightened little boy, that's who. A little Mommy's boy. Are you growing the nice little flowers for your mother, Ashe? That woman up there? That nasty woman. I don't care if she's sad. She's rude, and I don't like her. Go ahead, grow Mommy some flowers if you want.

—You done? I said.

—You gonna make her come outside? Is that it? You gonna get a little hug from your momma? I liked Will much better. He wasn't a scared little boy.

—Can you go now?

—You going to cry? Is that it? You need your momma?

I looked straight at her. The ground was swaying. I wasn't sure of my voice.

—*The flowers don't mind if you touch them,* she said.

I waited for her to leave.

—Do you think it's nice? she said. Having this . . . this bum leg and all . . . You tell someone something and they just . . . right back at you . . . spit in your face.

I looked down so she wouldn't see my jaw shaking.

—All right, I said. Can you leave?

—You were the one who—

—Can you just leave now? Please. Can you go?

She turned to leave, then she turned back.

139

—No. I'm not leaving, she said, and she sat down heavily on the grass with her bad leg straight out. I stood up to go.

—Don't walk off! she said, pointing at me. I've something to say to you. Look at me!

My head was trembling. It was hard looking into her face.

—I don't want a little boy, Ashe. I've no use for little boys. They're no good to me.

—Why'd you come here anyway?

—I really don't know.

—To tell me you hate me? Is that it?

—You think I hate you, do you? She shook her head and looked across the field. You don't know much, do you, Ashe?

She leaned over and stood up awkwardly on her good leg. Then she walked over and grabbed my hand and pulled me from the flower bed across the tall grass to the shed. She pushed me inside and came in herself, closing the door behind her.

—Take your shirt off, she said.

A thump of panic. I took my shirt off and dropped it on the ground.

—Now hold your arms out, she said.

I did as I was told.

—You can't touch me, Ashe. *Never.* Her voice was low, almost sad. You just can't.

I nodded.

She came over to me and traced her fingers around my chest, just her fingertips, around my nipples and arms and belly, then she rubbed me with her palms, stroking around my neck and under my arms and down my back, and across my waist. She touched my navel for a moment and stepped back, staring into my eyes, first the left one, then the right, then both. Her lips were quivering. It hit me all of a sudden.

—You *want* to. But you can't, I said.

—You're a real Einstein, she said in a low voice. She reached forward and brushed her hand down the front of my pants, and stood back. Her eyes were wet.

—*I like flowers*, she said, mimicking me. *They don't mind if you touch them.*

—I'm sorry, I said, and dropped my arms.

—What are you gonna do, Ashe? she said.

—What do you mean?

—With your life. What are you going to do with your life?

—I don't know.

—You've no idea? You told me once, remember?

—Become a merchant marine.

—You want to get away, don't you, she said.

—I guess.

—You want to get away from *her*.

I hesitated.

Yes, you do. You want to get away from her. Isn't that right?

—Maybe.

—As far away as possible.

—Maybe.

—*Maybe* is what a little boy would say. Do you want to get away from her or don't you?

—Yes . . . I do.

She came toward me and pulled my wrists down and pushed my arms behind my back, holding them there. She leaned in and took my lip between her teeth and bit down gently, sliding her tongue side to side on my lip, then biting hard. She let go of my lip and put her mouth beside my ear.

—That's what I'm for, Ashe.

I started to say something, but she held her finger over my mouth.

—Go outside, she whispered. Get some flowers, some of your mother's flowers. Three or four. Bring them back.

In a haze, I went outside into the light, the wind on my bare chest. I walked across the meadow to the flower bed. I picked some of the green buds and walked back. The door of the shed was closed and the blinds were drawn. I knocked on the door.

—One moment, she said.

My heart was racing. I stood holding the door handle.

—Come in, she said.

I went inside. The room was in shadow. She was lying on the bench with a bedsheet over her. Her clothes were in a pile on the floor. She'd moved the only chair in the shed beside the bench.

—Close the door, she said. Give me the flowers.

I handed her the buds.

—Now sit down.

I sat in the chair.

—You mustn't touch me. Just look into my eyes, all right?

Her eyes were looking right through me. I looked away.

142

—Watch my eyes, please, she said. My cheeks were hot. She smiled.

—It's all right, Ashe. I know it's hard for you.

She peeled the green buds until the tiny red petals were open, then she rolled them between her palms and rubbed herself slowly under the sheet. I watched her hands tracing over her body.

—Look at my eyes, she said again. Keep looking at me. I want to *see* you.

Her white face. The room was floating. She rubbed her arms, legs, belly, and slowly, her breasts, around and around. Then finally, between her legs. I watched her hands under the sheet from the corners of my eyes.

—Keep looking at me, she said. It's like *touching*. It's just like touching.

She moved with a steady rhythm. Her spicy smell filled the room, then she lifted her head in pain, crying out from a knotted throat, her body clenched, shaking all over. She was squeezing my hand. She lay back and looked at me again. I watched her eyes until her breathing was regular.

—*Ashe.*

—Yes.

—Can't you tell when someone loves you?

—No.

—You don't know much, do you?

—No.

She stood up and dropped her sheet. Two ample breasts, long dimpled nipples, tangles of pubic hair. She pulled me up and undressed me, then led me to the bench. I lay down and she draped the damp sheet on top of me and sat down.

—It's my turn, she said. Then I was stroking myself under the sheet, staring into her eyes, her flushed face right beside me, and as I started to tense, she reached across and held my hand and we stroked together.

—*Don't look away!* she said, her eyes right above me. My eyes closed when I came, her head was on my chest and she was squeezing both my hands as I spasmed in waves, twitching all over. When I stopped, I looked at her without shyness, like I was looking into a mirror.

She got up and found a towel and wiped me clean and sat beside me. I lay there empty, not a single word in my head. Then I slept. When I woke she was dressed, sitting beside me.

—You hungry? she said.

—Starving.

I put my clothes on and we went outside and across the field to the kitchen. I made her scrambled eggs and we ate them with green apples dipped in honey. When we finished, she ran her fingers through my hair. I was looking out at the trees, remembering the time I'd stood on a big branch with Will, high up in a tree. He was bouncing up and down to prove it wouldn't break. Then it broke, and we fell twenty feet onto the slope of a hill and rolled down head over heels, and he stood up with grass in his hair, giving me a look, eyes wide open, bottom lip pushed out, as if we'd just found money.

SHEILA FINALLY HAD to go. She kissed my neck and rode home on her bicycle. I didn't want to stay in the house. I went outside and sat under a tree waiting for Susan to come home.

I thought about Susan crying out in Nell's room, that animal groan of hers. You'd never expect from her such a sound. I imagined her sitting alone in some bar, and a quiet man sees her and sits down beside her. *Do you mind?* She shrugs and looks away. He starts talking to her, and she's brusque because she's shy, glancing at his face as she brushes the hair from her eyes, but he sees through that and stands his ground and makes her laugh, and then she talks to him, and he sees how different she is, and she sees that he too is different, and she opens up to him, and her years alone don't matter anymore because she'd never have met him without those years. Then they go away together and she's lying on a beach and the man is standing over her pulling her up, and she's hot and lazy and wants to sleep, but he won't give up, so she gets up and walks with him into the sea, and they dive together and swim under the water for a long time and come out in the sun-flecked waves and look at each other without talking.

17.

I WATERED THE flowers every day, and they grew tall and finally bloomed. On July first, I slid a piece of paper under Nell's door:

Dominion Day.
Black Rock Park meadow.
11:30 p.m.
Come and pick some flowers.

AT A QUARTER past eleven, I pulled a chair over from the shed and sat beside the flower bed. Her window was dark. She won't come, I thought. She won't. I watched the heavy clouds rolling in, covering the stars as it turned cold. The mosquitoes were everywhere. They blew away when the wind picked up. At one point a rustling started behind me in the grass. Raccoon or coyote, I thought. It wandered away slowly. Groundhog, maybe. Eleven thirty came and went.

I sat outside the whole night, nodding and sleeping. The rain started before dawn. It would stop eventually, and the sun would come out. I'd sit there until I was dry. Tomorrow I'd cut the flowers down with the trimmer. Or I'd snip them with the shears, just the heads. Or I'd pull them up and dump them. Or maybe not. It didn't matter. I'd decide in the morning. I looked up when the rain stopped. It was almost dawn. I held my watch to my eye. Four thirty, or was it five thirty? It must be five thirty, it was getting light. Against the white of the house, I saw someone standing a few yards away. I jumped up.

—Who's that?

—It's me.

—Who is it?

—It's just *me.*

It was Nell.

—What's wrong? I said.

—I wanted to see you.

I went over to her and ran my hand over her face.

—You came, I said.

She went to the chair and sat down. She had jeans on and a leather jacket. I stood in front of her and held her face to my chest.

—Don't talk like that, she said. Can't you get angry at me, for Chrissakes?

—You came back. It's all right now.

I squeezed a handful of her hair. I could see the waves pulsing over the grass. She dug her fingers into my hips.

—Don't treat me like I haven't done what I've done. Don't *pretend.* Please, I can't stand that.

—You came to me, I said. It doesn't matter anymore.

147

—It *does* matter, she said. It means everything. Think of what I've done to you. I knew full well what I was doing. Don't forget that, no matter what I say later.

I rocked back and forth with her, feeling her body against mine, hardly listening to her.

—I have to show you something, she said, I can't sleep until I've shown you.

—What is it?

—Will you come with me to see it? We have to go on a plane.

—On a plane? Of course I'll come.

—Don't talk like that. Why can't you be angry at me, for Chrissakes?

—It's all right now, I said. It's okay. It's over.

—It's not all right. It's not over. It will never be over.

—I forgive you, Mom.

She pushed me away and stood up. I tried to move toward her, but she kept her arms out.

—What's wrong? I said.

—I don't want you to forgive me.

—Why?

—I don't *want* you to. I want to feel bad, Ashe. Just let me feel bad, all right?

I sat down on the chair, suddenly tired.

—All right, I said.

She came up to me and I put my arms around her. She stroked my hair and held my head against her chest.

—We'll have to go, she said. We don't have much time.

—Go where?

—To the airport.

—But where are we going? I said.

—I'll tell you later. I've packed the bags. I put them in the truck while you were sleeping.

We walked through the field to the truck. She opened the passenger-side door and dropped the front seat, and I squeezed into the back. I used to sit in the front whenever we drove together, before the crash. She got into the driver's seat and turned on the cab light and took some lipstick from her bag, pursing her lips for the colour, then biting down and rubbing them together and tidying the edges with her nails.

—Don't worry. We'll be okay, she said. She started the truck and drove down the driveway. It'll be fine, you'll see.

At the road, she turned around.

—You all right?

—Yes, I said.

—I didn't know if you'd want to come.

—Of course I want to come.

—And don't worry, she said. We'll be fine.

—I'm not worried.

—I have to concentrate on driving now. I get shaky these days. She turned onto the road.

—They don't know about us going, Susan and Karl. They'd just make a fuss. You know how they are.

—Yes, I said.

—But I'll tell them later. I'll phone them.

—Yes.

—They won't understand.

—No.

WE DROVE ALONG the winding road where she'd carried Will. At the traffic lights I could see the tree where the car had crashed. It was covered with leaves. We turned south onto the main avenue that led to the highway. She drove slowly, leaning forward, gripping the wheel hard.

—We'll see a desert, she said, looking back at me. An amazing desert. We have to drive through it.

—Where is it? I said.

—California. Right beside Nevada. A real desert.

—Have you been there before?

—When I was young. I lived beside it for a time.

She had never told me about living beside a desert.

—With Susan?

—No, by myself. I'll tell you about it later.

—What's it like?

—It's flat and hot, just like you'd think, unbelievably hot. But it's dry heat, so at least your sweat cools you. You have to keep drinking, though. Every second you're losing water. People go for hikes and run out of water and then they're in trouble.

—What happens to them? I said.

—Sometimes they die, she said. It happens every year.

—Why are we going there?

—No, don't worry. We'll be okay. It's not dangerous if you're careful. There's something I have to show you.

—We're going there to look at something? I said.

—We're going there to *find* something. I'll tell you on the plane.

We drove in silence down the highway. We were moving slower than the rest of the traffic. The set faces of workingmen drifted by in trucks and cars as trees and poles flicked past. I didn't believe we were going on a plane to look for something. She was getting away from Susan and Karl, that was all, away from everything.

—What's in the desert? I said.

—There are plants and rocks and animals, like everywhere else, she said. It's not all sand dunes like you see in movies. You find bones everywhere from snakes and lizards and other things. You see them lying on the sand in little jumbles. It's a different world out there. It's so quiet. No crickets or birds. It's just the wind. And when there's no wind, you can't hear anything. It's like you're deaf. Sometimes you clap your hands just to make sure you can still hear. Every so often there's a car in the distance or a plane overhead.

—I like that—no sound.

—Maybe you're one of those desert people. Some people love the desert. I always thought it was a great gift to be able to love the desert.

—What about you, I said. Did you love it?

—No. I tried to, and I wanted to, but I didn't. I hated it in the end.

—What's it called?

—Death Valley, she said.

The name pulsed through me. I looked at her. Maybe she'd changed from all that time alone.

—A hawk, she said, pointing up. A brown hawk was gliding overhead with three black birds behind it.

—They're attacking it, she said. Have you ever seen that before? The birds disappeared overhead.

—No, they wouldn't attack a hawk, I said.

—You never know. Odd things happen.

As we turned off the southbound highway, the two lanes narrowed into one. The squeezing together of things, like in a funnel, the sloshing and swirling at the top, the surging and streaming at the bottom. And things went the other way as well, bursting outward, like water from a fire hydrant scattering wide across a street, wetting cars and dogs and children. The road opened onto the highway heading west toward the airport.

—It will be fine. You'll see, she said.

I imagined myself crawling over the desert sand with Sheila watching me from the shade of a tree. *Come back*, she was shouting. *Don't leave me here.*

A car honked from behind.

—You're in the fast lane, I said. You're going too slow.

—Just be *quiet!* Let me drive!

I sat back, feeling the insult, the disdain in her voice. How quickly she changed. The car drove by and honked again. The man was shaking his head. Another car honked from behind.

—You're going too *slow*, I said.

—I don't care. They can go around, can't they?

I felt the truck jerking and saw her arms were shaking.

—Let them go around! I said. Screw them! Go around! I shouted at the car. Is that so hard for you?

The car honked and passed us.

—We have to get into the far lane for the airport, I said.

—I can't. I can't move my arms.

—There are no cars, I said. I'll help you.

I put my leg over the seat to climb into the front.

—No! *No!* Stay where you are.

—Just *lean* sideways, I said. She leaned with her stiff arms, and the car veered across the three lanes and onto the airport road.

—I can't do it, she said.

—You just did. We're fine.

—I mean in the States. I can't drive in the States. I won't be able to. We'll have to call it off.

—Just keep going, I said. We can't stop here. The airport's up ahead.

—I'll be fine, she said. I'm not used to it, that's all. I'll stay out of the fast lane. When they're aggressive like that, I seize up. I'm okay now.

And then, a minute later, she said, I can't drive anymore. I've had enough.

—It's just up here, I said.

—It was a stupid idea.

We drove into the airport and around the winding roads and into the parking lot. She parked the truck and laid her head on the steering wheel.

—Goddammit, I'm tired, she said. I need to sleep.

—It's over now, I said.

I was tired too, and my clothes were wet and cold. I should have changed them before we left. I kept thinking, this isn't her, this isn't how she is. Why is she pretending?

—Clouds, she said.

—What?

—*Clouds*. I was thinking about bad luck, the way people say it follows you around, like a cloud.

—What about it?

—It's just, some people are bound to have bad things happen, aren't they, with all the people in the world, and all the things going on. You always forget about that, all those people running around, all the things they get up to. It's just chance, that's all. You have bad luck today and good luck tomorrow and bad luck the next day. There's nothing connecting them all. I mean, what *could* connect them? Why would the whole world put on a show for one sorry person?

—Yeah. Of course. It's just chance.

—But so many people believe it. Why do so many people believe it, Ashe? Why have people believed it right throughout history, in every culture? Why doesn't the idea just go away?

—I don't know.

—Listen, Ashe, you have to be careful, she said. Watch what's going on, watch all the time. Keep your eyes open.

—For what? I said.

—Just watch out. Be smart. Protect yourself. I've had bad things happen to me. You can't deny that.

—But you said there was no such thing as bad luck.

—No, there isn't. Of course there isn't, she said.

—What do you mean?

—I mean, there isn't such a thing, and there is. Both. At the same time. There isn't, and there is.

—Are we going or not?

—Should we? What do you think?

—Let's go, I said.

—You sure?

—Yes.

—All right. We'll go, then.

She looked worn out.

—You said you have to show me something there, remember?

—Yes. You're right. We'll go.

18.

WE LOADED THE suitcases onto a trolley, and I pushed them through the parking lot. She walked fast, with her head down, hugging the wall. In the terminal, passengers were rushing about. I saw a man and woman saying goodbye to a boy a few years younger than me. The man was crying; the woman was behind him looking embarrassed. The boy hugged the man, his face against his chest. They swayed from side to side. They pulled apart, and the boy turned to the woman and shook her hand. The man picked up a backpack from the floor and put it on the boy. It was too big for him. He walked toward the door at the back. The man watched him go. The woman was already turned away, looking outside. She was younger than him, with feathered blond hair and tight jeans and a white shirt with the bottom tied around her waist so you could see her smooth belly. As the boy disappeared, she pulled the man's belt with one finger. He turned and followed her.

Nell was over at the airline counter picking up the tickets. You see how Mom did that, I thought. You see how that worked? It's my trip now. She made me choose. She forced me. Did she force me? Is that what just happened?

She was so different now. She used to say things in a vague, open-ended way, like she wasn't quite sure that she was right, so it was easy to tell her she was wrong. But now her voice dropped at the end, like a schoolteacher's, like she knew something you didn't, and she couldn't explain it to you.

She came back with the tickets, and we lined up at the check-in counter. The woman in front of us held a sleeping baby, its mouth slack, its eyes tiny red slits in shiny pink skin. I wanted to touch the silky skin. An announcement boomed overhead, and the baby screamed. The mother held the baby's face against hers and sang, *London Bridge is falling down, falling down, falling down.*

The baby stopped crying and fell back to sleep.

—You were like that, Nell said without looking at me. You'd scream in the middle of the night and I'd go to you, but you'd be asleep when I got there. Then I'd go back to bed and you'd do it again, over and over ... that was you.

At the departure gate, there was a lineup of people boarding the plane.

—By the way, she said, I'm *terrified* of flying.

I wanted to ask her about it, but there were people around us. We showed our tickets and went through to the plane and found our seats. She was pale as the airplane taxied to the runway, her eyes shut tight, her hands gripping her legs. She might scream, I thought. What happens if she screams? I'd been on a plane once before, but it was different now. I was sweating and my stomach churned and my neck ached. I undid my seat belt and dug my heel into my foot until it hurt. I had to get up. I *had* to, but I couldn't.

ALAN GIBNEY

Nell started humming. The engines shook and roared, and the plane accelerated. Without volition, my body nestled back into the seat. The plane tipped up and we were off the ground, swaying from side to side. This second, I thought. Now. *Now.* Here it comes. The end. Falling, then nothing. Maybe you'd see something for a moment, the way you still see a room when the lights turn off, then nothing. As we climbed, the streets and buildings opened out into the arcs and blocks and grids of a map. Under the traffic sound of the rushing air was the rumbling drone of the jet engines. They didn't rise and fall like a car engine. They had no voice, no expression at all, they were purely mechanical and indifferent to flight, but they had to stop before the plane fell. I willed them to continue.

The plane banked so that the black and brown and green lattice of the city rose in the window. I waited for the free fall. Nell's eyes were clenched tight. It was her fear I felt, she'd given it to me. It wasn't there the first time I'd flown. That time, I'd looked out the window the whole way and laughed when we missed the landing and the plane bounced back up and had to land again. Now the light off the wing stung my eyes. A young girl was shouting in the seat behind us.

—*Mommy*, she won't sit. She doesn't like it. Look, she fall down, Mommy. Look! Princess! I can't find her!

She's scared, I thought. She's only pretending to play.

—Thank you, thank you, Mommy. I'll be good. I'll be good girl. Oh Princess, darling, where did you go? I miss you so much. Look, Mommy, she side up down. Isn't she funny. Side up down.

158

She sang a tuneless song to Princess. The words were all garbled. Shut up, I thought, just shut up.

—Not so *loud*, darling, her mother said.

I am bad luck. *Bad luck*. There's no such thing, she'd said, but there is, but there isn't. She sounded like an old woman. I'd never seen her that way. She didn't believe in luck. She never even used the word.

I thought of the wind blowing leaves at night. They rise in a mass like a flock of birds. You can't see them because it's dark, but you know what they look like tumbling over the grass, rising, falling, twisting, rolling end over end. You can mimic them with your hand. But wet leaves cling to the ground. Wet leaves and wet trees and wet grass and cold wind and dark clouds tell you that summer is over. You don't even want to look at wet leaves. You want to go inside.

The seat belt light went out, and people stood up to go to the washroom. Nell was sleeping. How could you sleep when you're so afraid? The young girl was in the aisle lining up for the washroom. She looked two or three. She smiled at me.

—Hi, she said.

—Hi, I said back.

She dropped her head and looked at me shyly from under her eyebrows.

—I'm pee-pee. I pee-pee to toilet. I'm big girl. Real big. She held her arms out showing me how big.

—That's *good*, I said. The girl's mother pulled her arm and they moved on. Beside me, Nell's face was loose, the face I'd imagined for

months. I stared at its curves and folds and shadows. She opened
her eyes and looked at me, then turned her head away.

—You all right? I said.

—I'm counting my breath, she said.

—Where are we going anyway?

She shook her head.

—Not now.

—You said you'd tell me on the plane.

—Give me a break, would you? I'll tell you later.

—I don't want to go to a desert, I said.

—We'll talk about it later.

—No, let's talk now.

She held her hand over her mouth and retched. I found a sick-
ness bag and gave it to her. She spit into it and held it over her face,
leaning forward. The people across the aisle were looking at her.

—Just leave me alone, she said through the bag.

After a while she leaned back, wiping her mouth on her sleeve.
I took the bag from her and tied it up and gave her a clean one. Her
eyes were closed again. She grunted as she breathed. Only a fool
would go with her, I thought, only a weak-minded fool. She's got to
tell me before we land. She can't force me to go.

I watched a stewardess handing out drinks in first class. Her
eyes were dark and tired. She was pretty but older, Nell's age. She
had a forced smile. When she stopped smiling, her face was sad. I
liked her dark eyes and sad face. You could talk to her, she wouldn't
pretend. But why was she sad? The same reason they're all sad,
women like that. Things didn't work out, the house fell down. I

and stood up and leaned into the wind with one hand on the tiller and the other hand on the side of the boat, the spray pelting my face. I hit a wave, and the boat jumped and my feet lifted off the floor and I slammed down hard with a crash. I stopped the engine and floated for a while, stretched out flat on the floor of the boat, the sting of the near miss draining through me. Then I started it up again and tore around the lake making sharp U-turns so I could ride the waves from my wake. I jammed the tiller out too fast and nearly tipped the boat over, and the motor shifted sideways so it sat at an angle instead of pointing straight down. I had to land on a beach and unscrew the motor and put it back in place before heading home.

There was something about that day I wanted to remember. I begged and begged Nell to let me go out in the boat. I was worried Will would come back and he'd have to go with me. The man who owned the boat was a guest of Nell's. He was old and frail with a grey beard that he kept stroking with his long fingers. He smiled a lot and spoke softly, sitting on the edge of his chair. He reminded me of an old parish priest. The two of us played checkers and he let me win. He didn't mind me trying out his boat. He'd lived by the sea his whole life and thought it was only natural for a boy to go for a spin in a boat, but Nell didn't like the idea. She wanted to go with me. I had to beg her in front of her guest. I promised to put on a life jacket and to stay where I could be seen and to not go over two on the accelerator and to come back in fifteen minutes. When I came back an hour late, Nell wouldn't talk to me, but the old man smiled and winked, so I sat with them, and Nell bunched up a napkin and threw it at me and told stories about Will and me, and the old man laughed and nodded as if the only boys worth their salt were ones like us. I remembered the dry freckled wrinkles across his face and the fan of folds anchored in his eyes.

There was something there, but it wasn't about the old man. It had to do with skimming over the waves with the wind in my face and the glinting hills and trees sliding by in the water. The whole world was a toy in my hand—the marbled sky, the winking sea, the ragged shore—the whole gleaming world was mine. I slipped down the winding rivers I imagined flowing across the lake, the engine wailing behind me. I could fly wherever I wished. I could glide through the miles and miles of tumbled clouds trapped in the water. I couldn't remember the actual feeling. It wasn't stored in my memory. I could only remember how easy it would have been to stretch my arm over the lake and bend the pine trees with my thumb and pick up the little island and fling it in the air and then reach into the water and catch in my fingers the very clouds that danced in the waves: how the whole living world was my body and my servant, and this feeling would last forever, through weeks and months and years, to the very end of my life, because I'd found the trick and opened the door, and I would never again have to feel trapped and empty. It's natural to think you can hold on to such a feeling, though it always fades and you're left with nothing. But for a time it was real, and I'd discovered it myself. And I'd never have found it if Nell had gone with me.

THE PLANE BEGAN to descend. Nell woke, and my fear returned. The wing looked fragile once again. Beneath us were brown hills carved by rivers that wiggled around like the cracks in a skull. The plane would burrow easily into those hills. What would it feel like falling out of the sky? A heart-snapping air-sucking burst of clarity—I'm going to slam into the ground, right here, right *now*. Falling, falling, falling, then nothing. Not even darkness, just nothing. You're not there at the end. Would you even feel the crash?

Nell was humming.

—What is it? I said.

—Don't talk. I've never done this before.

—You said you'd flown before.

—No, she said. They kicked me off the plane. Just . . . just leave me alone.

—You'll have to put your seat forward, said the stewardess with the dark eyes.

Nell fumbled with the button. I pushed it for her, and she leaned forward and gripped the armrests.

—You okay? I said.

—Just let me do this.

—You said you'd tell me where we're going.

—We're not going anywhere. Okay? I've changed my mind.

—Come on. You said you'd tell me.

—I just told you.

—Well, I'm not going with you, wherever it is.

—Be quiet, would you. Please be quiet.

—You just wanted to get away from Susan and Karl, right? That's what this is.

—That's right. That's all I wanted.

She turned away and I was back with the droning engines. The little girl behind was chatting to her mother. I thought, Tissue tissue we all fall down. What was that from? Round around the rosie. No, ring around the rosie, pocket full of posy, tissue tissue, we all fall down. The little girl too. The mother howls because her little girl's beside her, her little angel. The girl wails, *Mommy, Mommy, Mommy, what's wrong? Mommy, what's wrong?* Rosie, rosie, we all fall down. Would the mother tell her? That would be worse than anything, hearing the mother saying it in simple words. But she wouldn't tell her, she'd say, *Nothing's wrong, close your eyes, Mommy loves you, Mommy loves puddles.* But the girl would hear it in her voice. *Mommy! Mommy!* she'd scream. You'd hold on to her tight, to make yourself one with her. She won't feel a thing, you'd tell yourself, she won't know, it'll be over and she won't know. When it's over we'll go home, and I'll make her lunch and read her a story. (Will flying out the window. How loud did it sound when he hit the ground? Like nothing, after the bang of the crash, a sack of rice falling off a truck?)

Nell held my hand. I stopped concentrating on the engines.

—It's all right, I said.

—Tell me something. Her eyes were closed.

—About what? I said.

—About anything.

—You know the best way to listen to a song over and over?

—What is it?

—Every time you hear the song, that's one life, and when it's done, the life's over. Then you listen to it again, and that's another life.

—Keep going, she said.

—At the beginning of the song it's young, and at the end it's old. So you try to think of what it's like at the different parts of the song. When did it finish school, when did it get married, things like that—what happens here, what happens there. And when it's over you imagine it lying at its funeral. Each time you play the song you have to change the story.

—Are we close?

The runway was directly below us.

—We're right there, I said.

—Are we coming in straight?

—It's okay. We're fine.

WE TOUCHED DOWN, and the wing flaps went up and the plane shook and hissed to a crawl. As we taxied to the terminal, she said, *Never again.*

—Except for the way back, I said.

She was looking over at the couple across the aisle.

—Right, Mom? Except for the way back.

—Yes. Of course.

The plane stopped and we waited to leave. The light off the terminal windows hurt my eyes. I stood up and looked at the passengers around us. They were old and dressed in loud holiday clothes. One man was trying hard with gold chains and fake hair and bleached teeth. He was with a woman half his age who kept blinking when he spoke. He looked prissy, the way he fussed over his hair with his fingertips when she wasn't looking. I watched him until he noticed and looked back at me.

People were pushing their way into the aisle, straining for their bags. All this work getting on and off. It goes on day after day, the whole world over. All this scrambling about like rats in a sewer. It was exhausting to think of. We got our bags and lined up in the aisle, waiting for the door to open. I followed Nell out of the plane, up the ramp and along the passage to the luggage carousel. Through the dirty window, I could see the clustered palm trees and the khaki ground and the grey mountains.

—God, I hate this place, she said. It's a hovel. A real hole.

She wants to be cheerful with me, I thought, but she can't, and it annoys her she can't.

—We'll be gone soon, I said. You hungry?

—I must be. I haven't eaten in ages.

WE FOUND THE bags and took them through customs. The customs officer asked us why we were visiting Nevada, and Nell said we were there for the casinos. He asked me what I was going to do in the casinos.

—Follow her around, sir, I said.

He stamped our papers, looking at the next person in line.

—Welcome to Nevada, he muttered.

We went to an airport cafeteria and bought sandwiches in plastic wrap and coffee in paper cups.

—What will we do now? I said.

—We'll stay in town for a few days and go back.

—Is that what you want?

—It's all right. I don't mind.

Her lipstick was smudged at one corner. I cleaned it with my fingernail.

—You *sure?*

She nodded swirling her coffee.

—Your hair's a mess, I said. She tried to fix it with a pocket mirror, then she went to the washroom. She'd taken one bite of the sandwich leaving a red lipstick mark on the white bread. It looked sad lying on a paper plate. Her hair was down when she came back. Her black fringe matched the shadows under her eyes.

—Ashe, let's just get out of this *toilet*, she said. Imagine being stuck here with all these plastic people.

The people walking by had the weary, impassive look of travellers, stone-faced, smiling only at their companions.

—Were we really going to a desert? I said.

—It's all right. We don't have to.

—I know it's flat and hot, but tell me something else about it.

—A desert is a strange place to be, she said. There's no centre to it. It's like the sea, it just keeps going on and on and on. You're always looking at the horizon. There's only two places to focus, three feet in front of you and as far out as you can see. You're standing here but you're going way, *way* over there, and you have to keep on moving. You can't sit down, because it's too hot, and you know you won't be able to breathe if you sit down. You just keep walking. It's a kind of instinct. You're all restless, like there's something spinning inside you. You walk and walk and walk until you're out.

—It sounds pretty awful.

—It is awful, in a way. But there's something about it, too.

—Do you still want to go? I said.

—It's all right. I'm fine.

—But you were going to show me something, remember?

—Yes. That's why we came.

—Can't you tell me what it is?

—I wanted to *show* you, not tell you. I wanted you to come with me. I can't go by myself.

—All right. I don't mind. We'll go.

Her face darkened. She drank her coffee and turned the cup upside down.

—Well, I suppose that's why we're here. It's a four- or five-hour drive. We'll have to go fast if we're going to make it tonight.

—You think Karl will call the police? I said.

—Of course he will. They're his friends. He has to do something, doesn't he? I should phone them. I will phone them. I'll do it later.

—Susan will be worried, I said.

—I know.

—We should phone her now.

—Not now, she said. I don't want to talk to her now.

—I'll phone her, then.

She looked at me.

—What will you say?

—I'll say we've gone on a holiday, that's all. I won't tell her any-thing. You can listen if you want.

—All right, she said. Phone her if you want to. I don't need to listen. Dial zero and say you want to make a collect call.

I went over to the bank of phones and dialled the operator and gave her our number.

—Hello? Susan said.

—Collect call from Nevada, the operator said. Will you accept the charges?

—Yes. *Absolutely.*

—Hi Susan, I said.

—*Ashe.* Thank God. Thank God. Are you all right? Where are you?

—I'm fine. I'm with Mom.

—Where? Where are you? she said.

—We went on a holiday.

—Without telling us? The operator said you're in Nevada.

—Yes, we're in Las Vegas, I said. She wants to show me something.

—Jesus Christ, Ashe. Listen to me. You might not be old enough to understand this, but something is very wrong with your mother, very, very wrong. I don't know what it is, exactly, but you have to protect yourself. Is she there? Is she listening?

—She can see me. She can't hear.

—Right, you have to get her to come back home, she said. If she won't come, you have to get away from her and phone us. Karl will go down and pick you up. All right?

—I can't leave her.

—Ashe, please, *please!* This is not right, believe me. What is this thing she's showing you?

—I don't know, I said. It's in the desert. It's something to do with someplace she used to live.

—Nell never lived in a desert, never. She's never lived anywhere in America.

—She said she did.

—Believe me, she didn't. She's lying to you. She's lying. You've got to get away from her.

Nell was staring at me.

—Ashe, let me talk to her, Susan said.

I raised the receiver and pointed at it. Nell shook her head.

—She doesn't want to, I said.

—Christ. You've got to get her to come home, or you've got to run away.

—I understand.

—Will you do it? she said.

—No.

—Oh God, Ashe.

—I'm sorry. I have to go.

—Let me talk to her.

—No, I have to go.

—Phone me, she said. Please. Phone me tonight. I can't just sit here waiting for you.

—I'll phone if I can.

—Be careful. You're foolish, Ashe. You're very foolish. Please be careful.

—Goodbye.

I hung up and went back to her.

—What did she say?

—She wants us to go back.

—I told you she wouldn't understand.

—She wants me to phone her again.

—You see? She'd never have let us go if I'd told her. Come on, let's get out of here.

WE CHANGED SOME money and walked to the car rental stand. Nell lined up at the counter and I sat with the bags by the window. A man in a straw cowboy hat and shiny cowboy boots kept turning around and talking to her, waving a cigarette. She laughed and tried to look away. The man tipped his hat and let her go ahead of him and watched her as she leaned over to speak to the clerk. He could see I was looking at him, but he went right on staring at her ass. She searched her bag and handed the clerk some cards. The clerk shook his head and went off to talk to someone in the office. He won't let us, I thought. He won't let us. We'll have to go back. There's nothing else we can do. The man returned and gave her back the cards and started filling out a form. The cowboy kept staring at Nell with a smirk, rocking back and forth on his heels, the cigarette hanging from his mouth. The clerk gave her the keys, and we went outside and picked up our car, a white Chevy with a blue stripe down the middle.

—It's got a new type of air conditioner, she said. It's supposed to be good.

—Looks like a cop car.

I sat in the back and we drove into the city. I could see the signs of the casinos over the restaurants and shops. There was no grass anywhere, it was all red-brown dirt and bleached concrete. We stopped at a rundown gas station with an old taxi out front with the wheels missing. She bought a map and bags of salted peanuts and a case of bottled water.

—I can't breathe in this city, she said. We have to get out of this stench.

We drove onto the highway, past rows of houses with Mexican clay-tile roofs the colour of flowerpots.

—You're not scared driving? I said.

—No. That's gone.

I lay on the back seat and closed my eyes and listened to the tire hum. Watch her, I thought, don't sleep.

—You have a little nap, she said. I'm fine.

Don't sleep. Wispy lines cut across the sky. Not clouds, I realized, but airplane trails. Like skate marks across ice. Over the car noise I could hear traces of voices, schoolchildren, the customs man, Susan, my mother. Sleeping while moving was the best thing there was. *You have a little nap.* I liked the way she said it, like I was a kid. Have a biscuit, Ashley. Give me a cuddle. Out you go, enjoy yourself.

And outside, on the grass, my sweetheart is fast asleep, waiting for me.

19.

WHEN I WOKE, we were driving in the desert. The ground stretched flat on either side, clay brown and strewn with rocks. The rocks near the road snapped past in a blur, those farther off moved slower, as if the plain was spinning on a great disc.

—Why's it so hot? I said.

—The air conditioner's dying.

We rolled down the windows; scorching wind flapped through the car. On one side the mountains were far off and stationary, except for a scrap of cloud creeping behind the peaks. On the other side, they were closer and glided by as we drove; the shadowed creases of the rock flicked across the window frames.

—Is this the desert? I shouted over the wind.

—Yes, I didn't want to wake you.

The desert wasn't what I'd expected, just rocks and sand—a huge building site. My eyes jerked and fluttered, chasing the rocks.

—Where are we going? I said.

—What did you say? she shouted.

—*Nothing.*

It didn't matter. Whatever it was. When you finally see a thing, it's never much. It was an excuse anyway, this pretending we were here to find something. She wanted to get away, that was all.

—We're almost out, she shouted.

—How long have we been in the desert?

—Forty-five minutes. There's another half an hour to go.

She'd have driven clean across without waking me, after all that talk about the precious desert and how I had to see it for myself.

THERE WAS A lineup of cars ahead in the middle of nowhere. We stopped behind the last car. A man with a baseball cap was standing in the road holding a stop sign. His eyes were closed, and he was swaying back and forth. A board on the side of the road read ROAD WORKS, WAIT FOR ESCORT CAR. Two men were walking on the sand nearby, kicking rocks. One had a crewcut and a purple scar on his lip and looked like a soldier.

—Some travellers got trapped in here once, she said, a long time ago, before there were cars. Twenty wagons with horses and oxen. They had women and children with them. Young children. They thought it was a shortcut to the gold rush, but they got stuck here and ran out of water, can you imagine?

A patch of white flickered on the sand far across the plain. It was too bright for a mirage. A salt bed, I thought.

—When was that? I said.

—A hundred years ago, maybe. Something like that.

—Did they all die?

—Some did, I think. The rest killed their oxen for food and climbed out over one of those mountain passes.

—The kids died, I said, not wanting to know.

—No. They all survived. One of them was two years old. They all lived.

—How do you know?

—It's famous around here.

A truck with the word *Escort* on its grill drove toward us leading a line of cars. It pulled over and waited for the cars to pass, then it did a U-turn and led our line of cars along the road. We passed some men on the shoulder shovelling sand onto a pool of black fluid.

—What a mistake, she said.

I realized she was talking about the travellers with the children.

DRIVING THROUGH THE plain, I was drowsy with the heat, daydreaming about running toward my father as a kid. He was walking far up a beach. I was scared I wouldn't reach him and he'd leave without me, he was so far ahead. He was stretching away from me.

Pools of light quivered on the horizon, the hot ground swayed like heather, the same light flashing off the chrome waved gently on the road ahead of us.

I imagined Sheila beside me in the car, ignoring the heat and the useless sand, waiting for me to finish whatever I was doing so I could go back to her, fed up with my awful mother for stealing me away.

WE LEFT THE desert and drove over the mountain and across a narrow valley and then over a second mountain and down into the next valley. It, too, was a desert trapped between two mountain ranges, but it was slightly cooler and the shrubs were denser on the ground. We drove down the foothills and onto the desert floor. The shrubs flew past in a twisting gliding fabric that stretched across the valley. The car seemed to be moving faster now, closing in on something. The mountains ahead were dark blue and flecked with snow. They were too tall to drive over.

—Are we close? I said.

—Yes.

—Will we see it today?

—See what? she said.

—Whatever it is, the reason we're here.

She pulled off the road onto the sand and turned off the engine.

—What's wrong? What's wrong?

—Nothing, she said, and got out, walking into the scrubland, leaving her door open.

I followed her in the sudden quiet, the only sound a thin drone from a car in the distance. She sat against a telephone pole far back from the road and cupped her hands over her eyes. I stood in front of her, casting the same red shadow as the pole. Up close, the shrubs were wizened sun-scorched tufts, powdered with dust. A hot wind fluttered the ends of their cabbage leaves. Far off, a hawk was flying over the mountains. I looked for its shadow on the rocks, but it was too far away.

—Oh *God*, the sun, she said. I remember it now.

—Sit in the shade.

She crawled around the pole and sat in the shadow.

—Here. She patted the ground, and I sat beside her. A few crickets chirped with a dry pulsing sound, different from the crickets at home.

—We're close then? I said.

—It's just up the road.

—Let's go tomorrow. We'll go somewhere else today.

—We've come all this way, she said. I wanted to show it to you today.

—I don't care if it's tomorrow.

—This *heat*. She covered her face with her hands.

—We'll go tomorrow, I said. You can sleep today.

—I wanted to get there today, she said. I planned it out.

She crossed her legs and traced her finger on the sand, a round head, eyes and mouth. Fear was twisting in my chest. It mixed with the drilling sound of the crickets.

—I didn't meet Patrick after the war, she said.

—You didn't what?

—Meet Patrick. Meet your dad. It wasn't after the war, the way I told you. I met him before the war.

She was drawing lines around the face, waiting for me to speak.

—Before the war? I said.

—Yes. I mean not before the war itself—the war was going on when we met—but before he went away to it, before *his* war. That's when I met him, when I was seventeen.

—And then he left?

—Yes, then he shipped out. I knew him a short time and then he left.

—Should we go? I said.

—We met again when he came back, she said.

I was thirsty and my eyes hurt.

—Can you drive now?

—I can drive, she said.

We walked back to the car, the sound of our feet loud on the shrubs. We got back in and drove along the highway with the snow-covered mountains on one side and the brown mountains on the other. There were farmhouses scattered here and there, but the land seemed mostly deserted. We reached a town with a few stores. She stopped at a restaurant with a hand-painted sign out front, LA PALOMA—REAL MEXICAN FOOD.

—Is this the place? I said.

—No. It's farther up the road. We'll eat here first.

The restaurant was dark coming in from the sun. On the wall was a straw sombrero over a papier mâché bull. The tables and chairs looked like they'd been found on the side of the road. Two men were loafing at a table in the back with a line of beer bottles between them. By the cash register was a plaster statue of the Virgin Mary. Someone had put drops of glue under the eyes so it looked like she was crying. I could see fingerprints in the glue.

We sat at the counter and ordered burritos. The waitress shouted the order over her shoulder and leaned back against the wall with her arms folded behind her, staring out the window. There was nothing out there except the road and a few birds on the scrubland. Flies buzzed against a mirror along the wall, tapping as they hit. Overhead, the ceiling fan scraped as it spun, blowing the heat down on top of us. There was an old poster of a beauty contestant in a bikini and sash holding a CARTA BLANCA EXQUISITA sign. One of the men behind us belched, the other man cleared his throat and spat. *Exquisita*, I thought.

When the food came, Nell peeled open the tortilla and sorted the contents into three piles on the plate—chicken, beans, rice. She asked for a beer and the waitress gave her a bottle from the fridge and slapped a bottle opener on the counter and went to the kitchen. I could hear her talking in angry Spanish behind the swinging doors. She didn't like the person she was talking to. Nell opened the bottle and took a long drink and then ate the food in sequence, rice then beans then chicken, washing it all down with the rest of the beer.

—I was a waitress once myself, she said. Did you know that? That's where I met your dad.

I didn't want to talk about my dad. I didn't want to hear the way her voice changed.

—I served him twice before he spoke to me. We were complete strangers.

I bent my head and ate quickly, my tongue burning from the jalapeños.

—Should we go? I said when I was finished.

Nell paid in front of the Mary. The waitress gave her change without looking up. Nell put down a tip, and the waitress turned away, leaving it there.

—Quite the bitch, Nell said outside in the sun.

—I think she's angry at the man.

—Imagine the life.

We went back to the car.

—I think about those two meals, she said. How we didn't know each other then. I was seventeen and he'd just turned nineteen. He was waiting for his unit to be shipped out.

—Then he spoke to you? I said.

—Yes. The third time we spoke.

—What did he say?

—I can't remember. He was very funny though. I remember laughing a lot. He was a bit drunk, I think. He hated being in the army. He was so funny about it.

The valley narrowed as we drove, the rounded foothills rising around us. We came to a small town with six or seven stores, a few of them built in a pioneer style with false fronts and barrels by the door.

—This is it, she said.

We drove past the stores and turned into the parking lot of a shabby motel, just a row of wood cabins on a dirt lot, like a kids' summer camp. She went to the office to check in. I waited in the car with the door open. A bulldog crawled from under the office porch and walked toward me in the shade of the building, standing at the edge of the shadow. The ground was a red powder. I scraped at it with my foot. The dog stood watching me, then lay down just inside the shadow, the tip of its nose in the sun. Nell came out and we drove to a cabin and took our bags inside. She went into the bathroom and changed into shorts and a T-shirt and lay on one of the beds.

—Wake me in an hour, she said. Don't forget.

The door was open with the screen door shut. The dog walked slowly up the driveway to our cabin and sat on the porch in front of the screen door. I went into the bathroom and looked at myself in the mirror. I felt shy staring into my eyes. My voice was fake when I was with her, too fast and high-pitched, like an old woman meeting a friend in the street. Who talks like that? Some brilliantined boy with a part. *Enthusiastic*, that puke word, *enthusiastic*. A phony smile with pained eyes from the strain of pretending, tired mouth muscles, a tin laugh. Her voice was fake too, in a different way. Deadpan, dragging. A wood voice. Tin and wood, back and forth, back and forth.

The vanity had mirrors at the ends that opened inwards so you could see the sides of your face. I looked at myself in reverse. My face was crooked—the left lip was raised, the eyebrows were off, the nose was to one side. You couldn't see it when you looked straight on. Was that how I looked to others, all cockeyed? I peed against the porcelain. My urine was bright orange. I had to drink more water or I'd damage something inside. The liver, or was it the kidneys?

In the bedroom, Nell was asleep already, her mouth agape like an old woman's. The dog was standing at the screen door and lay down when it saw me, its paunchy muzzle covering its paws. I wanted to get water from the car, but I'd have to shoo the dog away and it would wake Nell. I lay on the opposite bed, facing her, not looking at her mouth.

I thought of a picture I'd seen in a book once, a bleached skull of a horse lying in the dirt. It was from a war or famine or something. The skull was grinning. They always grin, skulls. How would a horse die in the desert? Flat on its side, teeth clacking, eyes spinning. It raises its head but not its shoulders. A last few kicks and then it stops. What would that feel like? The very last push-up where your arms are shaking and you're too tired to make it up. You sink back and rest for a moment. At least, that's what you'd tell yourself—I'm resting for a moment. I'll try again later. Then you'd close your eyes and drift off.

She's planning something, I thought. Some gesture. Throwing Will's ashes in the desert. But there weren't any ashes. My throat hurt. The dog was still at the door. I turned away from her and faced the wall. The fan blew cold on my back.

20.

I woke to the dog barking outside the door. Nell was sitting on my bed in a white summer dress.

—I didn't want to wake you, she said. I wanted you to wake up by yourself.

—Is it too late?

—No, there's still time. I have to tell you something first. I was trying to tell you before.

—Tell me what?

—There's this house up the hill here. It's an abbey, you know, a religious order, with nuns. That's where I stayed, when I was here.

I sat up.

—You were a nun?

—No, I wasn't a nun, I just stayed there, that's all. I want to visit it again. That's why we're here. Nobody knew I was down here, you see. Not my father or my sister or anybody. I came by myself on a bus and stayed for six months and then I went back home. I never told a soul where I'd really been. I was just seventeen when I came.

—But why did you come?

—I was trying to tell you that, how I met Dad before he went away. I met him and we were together for a bit and then he shipped out to England. But then I had a problem.

—What problem?

—A *big* problem. I didn't know what to do.

—What was it?

—I missed my period. Do you know what that means?

I nodded.

—I couldn't tell my father about it. I couldn't go through all that. He was a career soldier and had just been injured in a training exercise and was going to miss out on the big war and he was very angry. I couldn't talk to him. So I went to our priest instead. He was the only one I could turn to. He arranged everything for me. It was against all the rules, but he helped me out. He knew someone down here and he arranged it all.

—You were *pregnant?*

—Yes, I was pregnant. I came here and I had a little girl. Your sister. Seven pounds, two ounces, a perfect little girl. And then I gave her away. That was all.

—I have a sister? Why didn't you tell me?

—I didn't tell anyone. I didn't even tell your dad. He saw the stretch marks on my belly and figured it out himself, but I wouldn't let him tell anyone.

—Why not?

—It was a secret, that's all. I gave away my baby, don't you see? I just gave her away. That's what I did, whatever the reason. If I had had the guts to stay at home, I could have kept her, but I ran down here and *gave* her away. She couldn't even sleep without me. She'd scream if anyone else picked her up. It was just the two of us and I left her with some strangers, because . . . well, because it was easier that way. Easier for me. I felt like I'd sold her for money. I didn't want anyone to know about it.

—She lives here?

—I don't know where she lives. The abbey's here, that's all I know. They'll have a record of her new family, I'm sure. That's why we've come. I want to find her. The Mother Superior did the adoption herself, she didn't trust the government. She put herself at risk for me. She made up a story about the baby and lied to the doctors and officials to get around the law. If she's still here, she'll know where she lives.

—But why didn't you try before?

—I told Patrick it was impossible to find her. He wanted to look for her, but I said I'd tried already; I lied to him about it. I told him she was someone else's now, we should let her live in peace. I didn't want him pushing me to look for her. I didn't know if I'd be able to find her. I didn't want to start the whole thing up. Maybe she didn't even know she was adopted. A few times I thought of coming here myself, but I never did.

—But you've changed your mind now? You want to find her now?

—Yes. I mean . . . I guess so . . . I guess I do. That was my idea anyway. I don't know what's happened to her, if she's even . . . all right. I don't know anything. But I thought we'd give it a try. She's twenty. She can make up her own mind if she wants to see us. She might be married herself, who knows. She might have her own kids.

—What's her name?

—I called her Grace. I don't know what she's called now.

—What if they won't tell you about her?

—They'll tell me all right. I'll worm it out of them. Just watch me.

I DIDN'T SAY anything as we drove up through the mountain pass. I wasn't sure about the story. It didn't seem right somehow. It sounded rehearsed, the way she said it. We came to a row of houses with picket fences; she stopped beside the last house, a three-storey brick building.

—This is it, she said. It's not much of an abbey. It's really just a house with some nuns living in it.

I opened the door to get out.

—No, you'll have to stay here, she said. They won't talk in front of you. Just stay in the car.

She walked to the front door and rang the bell. A woman in a grey habit opened the door and Nell spoke to her and went inside.

You have a sister. A *sister*. That's my sister over there. Look at her. My sister. Brother and sister.

Far up the dirt road, a thin dog walked toward me through the waving heat. When it was close, I saw it was a coyote. It was carrying something in its mouth. It sauntered up to the car and stopped a few yards away. It was a yellow tennis ball. It stared at me as if wanting me to play, then it turned and ambled into the scrubland. A little girl, I thought. She wouldn't make that up. Why would she? She wouldn't come all this way and lie about that. No one would. My own sister. She's sitting cross-legged on the grass. I reach down and pull her up. She's easy to talk to, easier than anyone, even Sheila. Long black hair down to her waist. A young woman by now. Her face, the same as mine but pretty. We'd be quiet together. We wouldn't need to talk. Just a word here and there. She'd understand how things are. We wouldn't keep looking at each other, because we'd know already. We'd stand side by side, facing the same things. It would be like breaking away from a noisy crowd and arriving home.

AFTER A LONG while, Nell came outside. She straightened her dress and walked across the garden and out onto the sidewalk, and then she wavered for a moment and sat down on the concrete. I ran over to her.

—No, no, she said. It was hot in the house, that's all. I'm okay.

—What's wrong? I said.

—No. I'm okay.

I took her by the hand and pulled her up.

—It's the heat, she said. I felt a bit faint just then. It was very hot inside. I'm all right now.

I helped her over to the car, and she sat in the driver's seat. I went around and got in beside her.

—It was stuffy, that's all, she said. All the nuns kept coming in and talking. And then they all took snapshots. Every nun had to have her own picture.

—Here, drink some water.

She drank from a bottle.

—The excitement, that's all. I was nervous, everyone asking me things all at once.

—But the girl, what did they say about the girl?

—They said a girl came here last year asking questions about her mother. She called herself Liv, and listen to this, she had different-coloured eyes, one brown and one green. That's what the baby had. It's very rare.

—What did she say?

—She said she heard she was born here, and she wanted to find out if it was true. They said they couldn't tell her anything because the Mother Superior was away and it was strictly confidential. They told her to come back later, but she hasn't yet.

—But she said she would.

—Yes. She said she'd come back. Maybe it's hard for her to get here, who knows. She didn't say where she lives. The original Mother Superior is dead, and no one else knows any of the details. They didn't keep any records after all.

—You gave them our address, right? I said.

—Yes, our address and phone number.

—Do you think she'll come back?

—She said she would. They told her they might know something about it all right, but they weren't allowed to say anything without the head nun being there. It must be hard for her to get here.

—It has to be her.

—It's her all right. She was the only baby that was ever born in the abbey. And she has those eyes. It's a very rare condition, only one in a million people have it.

—One in a million? I said.

—Yes, something like that. It's very rare.

—It must be her then.

—It's her all right.

—She'll come back, I said. You'll see.

—She said she would. They told her they could tell her something. If she wants to find me, she'll come back. I mean, she may just have wanted to know if she was born here, I don't know. Maybe the little they told her was enough for her.

—But she said she'd come back. Don't you think she will?

—It's up to her. At least she knows for certain she was born here.

—What's wrong?

—Nothing. Nothing. We should eat.

—Come on. What is it?

—No . . . it's just . . . I might have set myself up a bit. I might have had my hopes a bit too high.

—She'll come back, I said, don't worry.

—I got excited, that's all. I thought it would be easy. I thought we'd come here and we'd be able to meet her somehow.

—You *did* find her, Mom. She might not have come here at all, then you wouldn't know anything.

—That's true, she said. I just got too excited.

—I saw a coyote with a tennis ball in its mouth, I said.

—Where?

—Walking down the road.

—There's lots of them around here, she said. They go through the garbage.

—It stopped just over there. It stared right at me. It looked like a dog, like it wanted to play fetch or something.

She nodded, but she wasn't interested in a coyote.

—Let's get some food, she said.

We headed back down the hill. On the main road, she parked beside a sports bar with swinging saloon doors, and we went inside and sat on stools at a table in the corner. An old waitress with a man's raspy voice took our order. Her uniform was too tight for her grandmother breasts, the dry rumpled skin leaked out the top. We ordered barbecued ribs. Nell asked for a vodka and a beer.

—Tomorrow we'll walk in the desert, she said. There's a dry riverbed we can walk along. It's just like a road, so you can't get lost.

She took a long drink of beer. The mug was half-empty when she put it down.

—What's wrong? I said

—Nothing. Nothing's wrong. I'm tired is all. I just want to sleep. I'll finish this, and then I'll be able to sleep.

—Your eyes are red.

—I scorched them driving. I should have used glasses.

—What'll we do after the desert?

—We'll go home. I wanted you to find out about her. I wanted to give that to you. I couldn't just tell you in Black Rock. I had to show you, so you understood. I'm just tired now.

The beer was almost empty. She drank most of the vodka in

a single swig. When the food came, she tasted the ribs and pushed the plate away.

—Too salty, she said.

She picked at the potatoes with a fork and drank the rest of the vodka. She asked the waitress for another round and leaned her head on her hand, closing her eyes until the waitress brought the drinks. She drank the vodka in two gulps.

—Did they look strange, her eyes?

—No, it was subtle, one was slightly green and one slightly brown, a little darker than the other.

—Only one in a million people have it?

—Something like that, very rare. You could only see one eye when she was breastfeeding, so whenever I changed sides, a different baby would be looking up at me.

—Two different babies. Will would have liked that.

She turned away and looked out the window.

—Did you tell them about Will? I said.

She shook her head.

There was a young couple sitting at the bar. The man was talking to the bartender. He was worked up about something, talking fast, waving his arms around. The bartender was wiping the counter with a rag, not looking up at him. The woman was watching the television, tapping her glass with a key. She'd heard it all before.

—I have to have a wash, Nell said, still looking away.

—I'm done.

She waved for the cheque.

—It will be better tomorrow, she said. We'll see the desert. I'm tired now, that's all.

She was unsteady on her feet. I took her by the hand, and we walked to the motel, leaving the car in the road. Inside the cabin, she went to the bathroom and I lay on the bed. I listened to the water flowing in the sink. She was in her room again. I was outside in the shed. It wasn't disappointment she felt. That was a lie. It was anger. The water gushed in the sink full force, rushing and hissing as she washed. She was scrubbing herself clean. On and on and on she washed. Then the water stopped. I turned over and faced the wall. I thought, *A sailor went to sea, sea, sea. To see what he could see, see, see.*

The door opened, and she came out and lay beside me on my bed.

—Ashe, you awake?

But all that he could see, see, see ...

—Ashe?

Was the bottom of the sea, sea, sea.

She got up and lay on the other bed.

—I'm sorry.

Fuck off you're sorry. Tell the desert. Tell the sky. Sorry sorry sorry.

21.

In the early morning, I watched her as she slept, how she'd lie perfectly still for a time then start moving about on the bed, tugging at the sheets twisted around her legs, opening her eyes for a moment, then suddenly giving up and falling back to sleep. The gloom lightened gradually until the sun cleared the mountains and poured through the blinds, painting bright lines across her body, her face dark under the crest of light. She was still wearing her perfume. It mixed with the sour smell of the mattress. As the room heated up, I could smell the people who'd stayed there before, a locker room stench of underarms and feet rising from the carpet. My legs were aching from lying down too long. A car door slammed outside. An engine started. I got up and went to the toilet. The flush was loud, but she didn't wake up. She'd sleep for a long time yet, and she'd take forever to dress, and I was starving. I took ten dollars from her wallet and went outside.

The sun was strong though still low in the sky. The shadows were long and sharp on the red ground. I had a hollow feeling, like everything was fake, like the sun had just turned on an instant before, and nothing had yet started, and I could do anything before it started and it wouldn't matter, and at the same time, like the day was already set, and no matter what I did, I'd be at my limit before the end, right at my limit, fighting for myself.

Red dust coated the grass and weeds, sticking to my shoes and socks as I walked. There were dirty bottles and wrappers in the ditch by the driveway. The bulldog was lying beside the office. I knelt down and put out my hand. It looked at me and closed its eyes. I threw a twig at its belly. It raised its head and laid it down again. I stood up and walked to the road. It was a real hick town, just a few stores for the local farmers. I liked the wall of mountains beside the place. The rock face was so clear it seemed close, like you could hit it with a stone. There was a constant breeze blowing up the valley. A hammer drill started far up the road with a nice liquid sound. The dog was walking behind me, fifty feet back. I stopped and it walked over to a pole and left its mark and waited for me to continue. As I headed toward the corner store, I saw a girl serving coffee in a diner across the street. I walked over and went inside.

A group of men were sitting at a table in the back drinking coffee. They went quiet when I came in. An old woman was smoking behind the counter, reading a comic book. There were drawings of plates of food stapled to the wall. I thought the men were looking at me, but when I glanced over they were all staring out the window. I pointed at the ham omelette and the woman told me to take a seat. I sat by the door, as far away from the men as I could. Then I realized I was in their line of sight and felt them watching me. I turned my chair so I was facing the road. The whole place looked rundown and washed out, but it really was no different from my own town, just smaller. All towns look pointless when you don't live there.

The girl brought my food. She had red hair and a patchwork of orange freckles that ruined her face.

—Where you from? she said.

—Canada.

—Where are your folks?

—Sleeping, I said.

—You want coffee with that?

—All right.

She poured the coffee. Her breasts were low on her chest for a girl, soft hanging handfuls.

—Is this your town? You live here? I said.

—Not here. There's nowhere to live here, case you haven't noticed. It's just a road. I live on a ranch a few miles up.

—How old are you? Twenty?

—No. Eighteen, she said. Why do you want to know? How old are you?

—Eighteen, I said.

She laughed.

—Sure, lover boy. You're fifteen. Fifteen or sixteen. I have a brother your age.

She'd brought me the wrong omelette. It was filled with shredded carrots and mashed cabbage. The eggs were oily and overcooked. I held my breath as I ate. The splatter of orange spots spoiled her looks. Scrubland.

—Are you Irish? I said, trying to keep her there.

—Why do you ask?

—You look Irish.

—Because of my skin, you mean? She rubbed her forehead with her thumb.

—No, your hair, your red hair.

She traced her finger over her nose and down her cheek.

—My brothers have no freckles at all. Can you believe that? They're tanned like you.

—I have a friend with freckles like yours, I lied. She has orange hair and tons of freckles. She's from Ireland. I mean her grandparents were from Ireland. It's normal for them. They all have freckles there.

—Is she your girl?

—I guess so.

—You've got a girlfriend already?

—I guess so. What about you? Have you a boyfriend?

—What's her name then? she said.

—Sheila Meegan.

—That's Irish all right.

—I know, I said. She has lots of freckles, more than you.

—It's the sun here. It makes them really dark. They wouldn't be bad if there wasn't so much sun. Is it hot where you are?

—Only in the summer.

—It's always hot here, every day. My brothers don't have any freckles at all, like you.

She ran her finger down my nose, it tingled in my legs.

—She's different from you though, I said.

—Who?

—Sheila, my girlfriend. She's different from you.

—How's she different then?

—Well, she likes her freckles. She likes her skin. She thinks it makes her look different.

—Yeah? Freckles. She likes them, does she? A little girl was in here and said, *Mommy, Mommy, she's got* paint *on her face.* You know, like someone flicked paint on me. She was only two or three. She probably plays with paint. A smart little girl. *She's got paint on her.*

—Well, Sheila's the same. She has more than you, but she likes them. She wears browns and greens, solid colours. She looks good with freckles. Healthy.

—She lives near you?

—She lives on a farm nearby, I said.

—You're a country boy then?

—I guess. I live in the country.

—In Canada, she said.

—In Ontario, Canada. Ontario's a province. It's just like a state, like California.

—So you like freckled farm girls then, do you? What's your name?

—Ashe, I said.

—I'm Lynn. So you like farm girls with freckles. But I'm too old for you, I'm eighteen. You think I should cut my hair?

—A little maybe.

—I probably need to. She played with her hair, looping it around her finger.

—Just up to here, I said, touching her shoulder. She moved with the contact. She was shy. You couldn't tell from her voice.

A bell rang in the back, and she made a face and went to the kitchen. I ate the oily eggs, thinking about her wanting a boyfriend. I caught her eye across the room, and she smiled and gave me a pout. Once your eyes adjusted to the dark, her freckles didn't seem so bad. I imagined kissing her on the nose and forehead and holding her face against my face, lying in the sun, lying beside her on a beach. Would she have freckles everywhere? On her belly? On her thighs? Between her legs? The skin would be smooth against your lips, even with freckles. I didn't mind the freckles. Cherries in a cherry tree.

—You coming back? she said, bringing the bill.

—Maybe.

—I'm here tomorrow.

—I'll come back then.

She laughed and said, Lover boy. You're older than you look. We'll talk tomorrow.

Walking back, I imagined leaning into her as we sat together. I'd take her down to New York and we'd walk through Central Park and talk about her problem. I *like* your freckles. *Yeah?* You do? Well, you can have them if you want. She had a round flat face, but nice. Like Shirley Temple. A strong healthy body. Thick muscles in her legs, but not too thick. She stood out from other people. They'd like her in a place like New York where everyone wants to be different. Anywhere but a hick town.

In the cabin, Nell was still asleep. I took a folding umbrella from her suitcase and sat outside on the stairs with the umbrella up. I thought about the freckled girl phoning me up one day, telling me she'd travelled a long way to see me, that she *has to* see me. Then we'd be alone together in an unlit room. She'd be embarrassed and shy and wouldn't look at me. I'd say, it's all right. I don't expect anything. I'm not like that. Just look into my eyes. I just want to see you.

A bowlegged man in dirty jeans hobbled over and said it was well past check-out time, were we planning to stay another night, and didn't we think of telling the office? I said I thought we were staying but I wasn't sure, my mother was asleep.

—Something wrong with her? he said, gobbing on the ground.

—She's tired, I said.

—I can see that. Tell her to come over when she's up. She'll have to pay for another night, like it or not. That's the rule.

—She'll pay. There's no problem with that.

—There's someone asking for her. I'll send her over.

Fucker, I thought. Then I saw how his leg was dragging and his arm hung down. *Stroke*. That's why his face was twisted. To be paralyzed here, in this wasteland. No flowers or grass. The ground grey and brown, brown and grey. He looked lost, vacant, like he was only half there, like every other cell in his face was missing. His eyelids hung down so you could see the red flesh underneath. He probably didn't even care he was about to croak. How would you dig a grave here? The ground was too hard. You'd need a road drill.

A woman in a grey habit walked over from the office with a crucifix hanging at her side.

—I'm looking for Nell. Is she here?

—She's inside, I said. She's asleep.

—I don't want to wake her if she's sleeping. I'm an old friend of hers. I'm Sister Martha from the abbey. I was away when she visited. I was hoping to meet her. I thought she might have left. Are you staying for a while?

—For another day, I guess.

—I'll come back then. Are you . . . may I ask . . . are you related to her?

—I'm her son Ashe.

She sat down suddenly on the steps.

—It's *hot*, she said. I never get used to it, even after thirty years. You'd think you'd get used to it after a while. I shouldn't have walked so far.

I fetched a bottle of water from the car. She drank with pursed lips like she was sipping from a wine glass.

—Do you have any brothers or sisters? she said.

—A brother. But he's not here.

—Two sons? That's wonderful. I knew your mother long ago, when she lived here during the war. Did she tell you about me perhaps? Did she ever mention Sister Martha?

—No, I don't think so.

—No? Of course not. Why would she? It was a long time ago. We've all moved on. It was twenty years ago, during the war, a long time. But I never left the convent. I live in the very same room as I did back then. A bed and a bookshelf, that's all I've ever had. And a . . . what do you call those things? Beside the bed with a drawer? A night table. That's all. And a few books. I'm still there. Nell's room was right across from mine.

—Do you want me to wake her? I said.

—No, no, let her sleep. It's difficult for her. I know that. I've thought about her every day for twenty years. I've prayed for her every single day. Twenty years really doesn't seem such a long time now. You probably wouldn't understand that, a fellow like you, a young strapping lad. But for me, doing the same things day after day, it's not such a long time, really. I remember her very well. Tell me, does she still go to church?

—No, I said.

—No? I suppose I'm not surprised. But does she still believe?

—No. I don't think so.

—That's sad. That's very sad.

—You were friends when she was pregnant?

—Yes. Good friends. I was with her the whole time. I was there when she had her baby. I helped in the delivery. I was trained as a nurse, you see.

She rubbed her eyes and then got up.

—I'm going back now. Please tell your mother I was here. Sister Martha. Don't forget, okay? Tell her I heard about her visit and I'd love to talk to her. I'll be going to nine o'clock mass tomorrow morning. Can you see the church? Through the trees there. I'll wait for her after mass, quarter to ten. But if she wants, she can drop by the abbey any time.

—I'll tell her, I said.

—Don't forget now.

—I won't.

I walked up the driveway with her to the road, holding the umbrella over her head.

—Here, I said, giving her the umbrella.

—You'll need it yourself.

—No, I won't. You can give it back tomorrow. Maybe you should get a ride up the hill.

—I'll be okay, she said. Tell your mother about tomorrow, okay? It's Sister Martha.

—You're going to walk up that hill?

—I'll be fine.

—You should take a taxi.

—No, no. Goodbye.

She walked up the road and turned in to the church. Heading back, I could see the cabin blinds were up. I knocked on the door.

—The motel guy says you have to pay for another day, I said.

—I'm changing.

—I had breakfast in the diner. Can I come in?

—Wait.

—You have to pay for the room, I said.

—Yeah, yeah.

She came out dressed in khaki pants and a shirt.

—We have to hurry, she said. You go change. Make sure you cover up your legs and arms or you'll burn. I'll pay for the room and get some things.

She walked over to the office.

I changed my clothes and lay on her bed. She'd whined in her sleep. What was that about? If only this, if only that, things that couldn't be changed. She was riled up again, riled up and certain, with an edge in her voice. She was physically strong, a soldier's daughter. She had wiry arms with tight ropy muscles. You could see the veins when she lifted something up. And she was strong in another way, she never gave up once she set her mind on something. Even when she gave up, she did it harder than anyone else—months and months alone in a room. You could never win a fight with her; you were always too tired in the end. I have to go because I planned to go. That was her logic. We must because we have to. Even if we hate doing it. We'll go to the desert, then we'll go back home. It'll be like we never left.

Suddenly, I wanted to talk to Sheila. I picked up the phone by the bed, but there was no dial tone. Nell parked the car in front of the cabin and honked. She had a pair of sunglasses on and a tight frown. I grabbed an ashtray and flung it at the wall. I hated that face of hers. I went into the toilet and brushed my hair and stared at myself. You never smile or frown at yourself in a mirror. You're always dead serious. Your real face. I'm going with her, I thought, that's all. End of story. She honked again, and I went outside and got into the back of the car.

—I've got sunglasses for you, she said. And look, I bought a hat. Let me see it on you. It's called a panama. It was the biggest size they had, see if it fits.

I put the hat on, and she laughed, adjusting the rim.

—You look so serious. Little Ashe Finder, attorney-at-law. We're just going for a walk, don't you want to go?

—I've got a headache.

—It's the dry heat. You didn't drink enough. Take an Aspirin, here.

She handed me a tin of Aspirin. I took two and drank some water. The pills stuck to my tongue, filling my mouth with a bitter taste. I washed them down with a second swallow.

—I talked to a guy at the gas station, she said. He showed me where to go. It's well worth seeing.

—There was a nun here looking for you, I said.

—Did she say her name?

—She said Sister Martha.

—My God, *that* woman? I thought she was long dead.

—She wanted to talk to you.

—Don't worry about her. She's a bit strange in the head. They look after her at the abbey. She has nowhere else to go. She walks around all day bothering people. What did she say to you?

—She said she helped deliver your baby.

—Jesus Christ, she's a crazy old bat, don't listen to her. She didn't help deliver the baby. She's a real nut, that one. She tried to breastfeed my baby once. Can you imagine? She was always picking her up and walking around the house with her, and one time I went into the bathroom and there she was with her breasts hanging out and the baby sucking on her nipple.

—*Gross.* What did you do?

—I grabbed her away and told her never to touch her again, and she said she was just trying to help out. She couldn't understand why I was mad. She didn't think she'd done anything wrong. But the nuns were all aware of her. They told me she'd turned strange over the years.

—She didn't seem strange, I said.

—Believe me, she is. Don't talk to her again, okay?

—All right.

WE DROVE THROUGH the town and out onto the highway. The droning of the road mixed with the pain in my head. I didn't want to talk. If we started talking now, we'd talk the whole way, one thing following another like a string of handkerchiefs pulled from a hat.

There was something odd about that nun all right. Twenty years of prayer for Nell, and going out of her way to tell me about it, like it gave her a claim, like Nell owed her something. And the way she prattled on, the way she stared at me with her mawkish eyes. What did she want? And why squeeze my arm so tight? Yes, lady, you knew my mother, I heard you. Twenty years of praying, her thumb pressed hard into my arm. It was too much. Why not let me wake her up if it was so important? Why assume I wouldn't give her the message?

We drove down the same highway we'd driven the day before; the scrubland swept along beside us. It was soothing, except we'd have to come back again, so it all seemed somehow pointless, like we were going in circles.

ACROSS THE SILVER edge of the door, light flickers and flares. Light hovers over the ground and pools on the road. Light grows in the open fields, bursting and shimmering, it rises in plumes. Up, up it rises, back to the sun. Pushed and pulled. The white fields bending in light. I imagine myself lassoed around the waist. I fall onto the sand squinting with the dust and glare. I'm dragged into the old house, through the ballroom, up the stairs, down the hall to the master bedroom. I'm thrown onto the bed. I try to escape but can't get away. I'm stuck to the great man's bed. But suddenly it's no longer just the house anymore. Outside, standing on a hill is a girl. She's waiting for me. At first she has a blank face, then she has a changing face, a thousand different faces, each with mismatched eyes. I wave at her from the bedroom, but she doesn't move. I imagine holding her hand, her dress flapping against my leg. Then up she flies into the wind and I'm holding her by the arm and she's shouting, *Hang on, brother, hang on, don't let go.*

22.

THE CAR OVERHEATED in the mountains and we had to trundle up the steep road in first gear like a roller coaster grinding up the lift hill. Then the air conditioner broke with a thump, releasing a stream of engine heat into the car. We rolled down the windows, and the hot desert air spilled in. I leaned forward from the back seat, my head beside hers. It was too loud to talk with the pounding wind. I felt close to her in the noise, not being able to talk. We drove down the foothills and onto the desert floor and turned onto a dirt road that ran between two broken fences. The posts were still standing, but the crossbars lay in pieces on the ground.

A few hundred yards down the road was the place she was looking for, an old abandoned campground. We drove around the empty campsites and parked at the edge farthest from the road and ate the food she'd brought: bread sticks, cheddar cheese, salted cashews, and mandarin oranges. The picnic tables were slumped over. There were shrubs and weeds everywhere. Nell stared out her window as she ate. She'd had hours to think while she drove, and she was still thinking.

—So what's here? I said.

—It's the riverbed. It goes for miles. We'll walk along it and see the desert.

—Where's the water gone?

—It's all dried up, she said. It only flows for a short time in the spring. But you'll be able to see where it flowed. The sand is shaped by it.

We each carried two large bottles of water in plastic bags and headed out onto the rutted scrubland and down onto the wide gravel riverbed, with its long curved channels of smooth clay, dried and cracked into tiles. I picked up a piece and crumbled it into dust. One side of the riverbed was a steep cliff of rock and clay thirty feet high that cut through the foothills of the mountain towering beside us. The other side, fifty yards away, was a low wall of layered sediment five feet high, topped by the desert plain, which stretched across the valley to the far mountains.

—Up here, Nell said, pointing away from the campsite.

In the quiet, her words were loud and close, as if we were in a small room. When I stood still, my ears churned on the silence. When I walked, I could hear the phantom seashell sound of distant surf under the steady scuffing of our feet. There was nothing but shrubs and sand and stones. It wasn't unimaginable heat, the way she'd said. It was just ordinary heat, like standing in a parking lot on a hot day, the sun reflecting up into your face. I dropped behind her, walking in her tracks. She'd said we were heading toward a bank above a fork in the river, but the view never seemed to change.

Turns out I wasn't a desert person after all. It took me less than a minute to figure that out. I had no interest in this place. I didn't need to see any more. She was striding ahead of me. My shoulders were baking hot. It was hard to catch my breath. Wind fluttered at the edges of my sunglasses, hurting my eyes. But it wasn't as tough as people made out. If you took it slowly and didn't drink too fast, you could walk all day if you had to. I lifted my hat and my head felt cool for a moment, the hatband drenched with sweat.

SHE WAS WALKING too fast, pulling away. It was hard to judge just how fast. Her legs were bent in a liquid mirage. At some point she wouldn't hear if I called. She knelt down to tie her shoe and glanced back at me. I raised my hands, but she didn't see. She was half a football field away, maybe sixty yards. She was racing ahead. A lizard ran across my path leaving little dents in the sand that faded in the wind. There were holes around the shrubs where the snakes and lizards slept in the ground, waiting for night.

Some people love the desert, she'd said, but that was crap. If you're in a desert, you know it's crap. No one loves a place where the rocks are too hot to hold. It's just something people say. *Look at me, I'm this, I'm that, I'm the other. I'm a magic seer with a mystic soul. I went to Arizona and fell in love, simply fell in love with the desert, the sacred, elemental desert.* It was all crap.

Clouds passed overhead now and then, sweeping brown shadows over the ground. I turned my back on her and urinated on the sand. A sad little mound. It dried up right away. There's no end to this. Where does this end? I ran toward her for a few steps and stopped short.

—*Hey!* I shouted.

She turned and I held up my hands. I couldn't make out her face in the distance. She pointed at something ahead and squatted down, waiting for me. For Chrissakes. Is this not enough for you? You need more? I tied the plastic bag to my belt and took it slow catching up to her, no extra movements, no anger. Let her roast.

—It's just over there, she said. I'm pretty sure.

—Let's go back.

—You want to go already?

—It's too hot, I said. There's nothing here, it's just sand. Look at it. Let's go.

—We're almost there. It's around that corner. We can climb up the bank and look at the view. Here.

She held a water bottle to my mouth. I drank the hot water and we walked on.

—It's a real honest-to-God desert, isn't it, she said.

—If you say so.

—What do you think of it?

—Hot, I said.

—It's amazing though. Isn't it worth seeing?

—We've seen it.

—Come on. We're almost there.

The scorching wind stung my face, making it hard to breathe. Drinking didn't seem to help. The water was too hot. I had to force myself to swallow. We reached the place she'd pointed to, but there was no fork in the riverbed.

—It must be up ahead, she said, just past those rocks, not far.

As we walked, the rocks jogged up and down without getting closer like we were standing still.

—It's just up here, she said again, after a long time. Just a bit farther.

I let her go ahead of me.

You make yourself wiry in the sun so the heat slides off you. You're just staying alive out here. You're the last man alive. Walking and walking for days on end, you come across a bundle on the ground. You go closer to it and it's a young woman. You push her with your foot. She's still alive. You give her your hat and pick her up and carry her on your back, your hands holding her bony thighs. She's crying because her man's gone, everyone's gone. Hold on, miss, you say, I'll save you. She's inspecting you now as you walk, a good strong horse this one, she thinks. I'll take this one instead.

It wasn't parking lot heat, it was more like an emergency tone, a broadcast signal, but still off in the distance. There were weeds everywhere, too thin to hold the desert heat, like water bugs, too light to break the water's surface.

After a long time, we reached the split in the riverbed. It was nearly two hours since we'd left the car.

—Up here, she said, pointing up the bank, a steep incline of loose sediment thirty feet high.

We climbed up on the heavy boulders embedded in the gravel. At the top was a rocky plain sloping up to the brown buckled mountains. We sat on a pair of boulders and looked down over the valley. From above, the flow and eddies of the river were clear. There was a twisting path of white silt in the centre of the riverbed, like the underbelly of a snake, that shone in the sun and seemed like the river itself still flowing.

—What's that? she said, pointing up the hill.

—A house? I said.

—Maybe . . . Let's take a look. Come on.

It didn't seem far at first. We climbed up toward it, our feet slipping on the gravel and rocks. Then the climbing became hard. We stopped halfway to rest. Sitting on the scalding sand, I closed my eyes for a minute. You'd get used to even this, I thought. If you did it every day, it wouldn't be anything, it wouldn't scare you at all. I could see the shape clearly now. It was an old wooden cabin. It had two empty windows like eyes. I didn't like the look of it.

—It's just a shack, I said. Let's go back.

—We're almost there. Come on, I just want to see it.

The valley broadened out behind us as we rose, an endless clay floor hedged in by mountains stretching down to the horizon. In the distance were the salt beds, like great white lakes. I could hear my pulse as I climbed. You'd get used to it. People live in deserts. Their bodies adjust. All you'd need is shade for half an hour and you'd be fine. She was tough though. I'd give her that. She was a lot tougher than she looked.

—It's an old miner's house, she said.

It was no more than a large wooden box with a sloped roof. It was big for a cabin; that's why it had seemed closer than it was. The planks were thick and roughly hewn and tar-stained, like railway ties. You could see the heavy iron nails they'd used to build it. There were clusters of hammer marks around the nails. Most of them were bent and banged flat. Through the door, I could see white objects littering the floor. Short white objects. Like ivory. I approached the window, my hand over my mouth. Bits of white wood were strewn about on the floor, broken slats from the rotting ceiling. I felt sick.

Nell went inside the cabin and pushed the wood around with her feet, and then she sat on the doorstep. I picked up a stone and threw it at a mound of rocks nearby.

—*Don't!* she shouted. Not at that.

—Why not?

—It's a grave.

—How do you know? I said.

—That's how they buried people up here, just a big pile of rocks like that.

I went over to the mound.

—Are they always like this? I said.

—Up here they are. They just cleared a spot and put rocks on top of it. You can't dig a hole here.

—There's a skeleton under there?

—Probably.

I squatted down, my hand over my eyes against the glare. It would take hours to build a mound like that. The big rocks would be hard to find. You'd have to walk a long way and carry each one back by hand. They'd probably done it early in the morning, when it was cool. But why make it so close to the house? The body must have stunk through the holes. They must have covered it with sand first.

—Why did they live up here? I said.

—They'd have found some gold or silver or something. They were probably mining it. There's sure to be more houses nearby. Probably over the ridge.

I looked up the hill but I couldn't see anything.

—We'll go home soon, she said.

And the way she said it, I knew she'd planned to come here all along and that she'd been lying about just wanting to see the desert.

—Why did we come here? I said.

—I thought you'd like to see it.

—*Look at me.* Why did we come here? You knew this place was here.

—No, I didn't. I mean, of course I knew there were cabins around here, but I didn't know about this one.

—Tell me why we came.

—Ashe, what do you want from me?

—You're lying, I said. Why did we come here?

—Christ, *Ashe.* Stop it, would you?

—Tell me.

She turned from me and looked down the valley.

—She's not going to phone us, is she? I said. She doesn't want to find us. Tell me the truth.

She looked at me for a moment.

215

—All right, she said. I don't think she does. I don't think she wants to. It didn't sound that way.

—Why didn't you just tell me that?

—I didn't want to tell you.

—You could have told me. It wouldn't have mattered. I don't know her.

—I didn't *want* to, do you understand? It's something to do with me, not you. I don't mind you knowing, I just didn't want to tell you, that's all, to say it out loud. *Jesus Christ.* I shouldn't have taken you here. There's nothing for you here.

—Shouldn't have taken me where?

—To this place. This country. It was a mistake. There's nothing for you.

She stood up, facing the cabin, her back toward me.

—It isn't so bad, Mom. It doesn't matter.

She went inside the cabin.

—It's just too hot, I said. We'll go back now, come on.

She was picking up the wood slats from the floor.

—When you've lived for a while, she said, you'll see how everything keeps repeating itself. You get to the end and you start again and you get to the end and you start again, over and over. Everything keeps saying, look at me, aren't I good, watch me, you're not watching, see how good I am. But you've seen it all before. It's just repeating itself over and over.

She started stacking the slats by the wall.

—What are you doing? I said.

—I'm tidying up, aren't I? If this was your house, out there would be your front yard, and beyond that would be a desert. You'd want more than this hovel, wouldn't you? You'd want so much more.

—Mom, should we go back?

—No, I'm cleaning up, I'm tidying. The nuns asked me about going to church, can you imagine that? Do you still go to church, Nell? Do you still confess?

—Mom . . .

—Like I've ever gone to church. Stand, sit, kneel, stand, sit, kneel, *amen.*

—Mom. *Stop.*

I went into the cabin and took her by the hand and led her outside.

—I'm sorry, she said.

—You can't clean up, Mom.

—What if I was to stay here?

—You can't stay here. We have to go.

—I used to watch you through my window, do you know that? Through the dirty glass.

—I know. Come on. I pulled her hand and we walked side by side away from the cabin.

We followed our trail down the mountain. Our footprints disappeared in the rocks and gravel.

—It's down here, she said.

—No, it's over there, I said pointing farther up the bank.

—I'm sure it's this way. Anyway, it's all the same. We'll hit the riverbed. You can't go wrong with the riverbed.

—But when we climbed up you pointed that way. It must be over there.

—No, remember, it was a cleft in the bank, she said. We were facing to the right when we climbed up, that's why it seemed like I was pointing that way.

She acted it out, showing me how you could get confused. She was sure and I wasn't, so I followed her down the slope. We came to a patch of sand that we hadn't crossed before. It was wide and smooth, without footprints. We were going the wrong way, but it was too hot to argue about it. We'd hit the riverbed soon enough. It would just take longer to walk to the car. I let my weight carry me down the hill, my eyes following her wavering shadow.

I thought of swimming with Will in the sea, how we once got caught in a current heading back to shore. I screamed and screamed at a boy on the beach, who stood up and stared at us for a while and then gave us a lazy wave and walked up the sand to the parking lot.

—Just keep swimming, Will yelled. We swam as fast as we could and slowly made it back to shore. I was ashamed of screaming. I couldn't explain it away. You can always tell panic when you hear it.

WE REACHED A cliff that dropped forty feet to the scrubland. There was no riverbed there, just a vast desert plain stretching out to the foothills across the valley.

—It must be behind that ridge, she said, pointing over the plain to a rise. The river must have a bend. You were right, we went too far. We'll go down here and walk over until we find it. It must be there.

—No, listen, Mom. We've got to climb back up and go farther down the other way, where I said. We have to find the riverbed. It's back there somewhere.

She was staring down at the plain.

—I don't want to climb up again. (A slight whine, like the whine of a child.)

—We can't play around, Mom. It's not a game. Look at the house. You didn't point that direction, you pointed over there. We're facing the wrong side of the house. The river has to be back there. It has to. We have to find it. We can't go wandering around the desert.

—Okay, calm down, we'll do what you say. Whatever you think.

—Do you have any water left? I said. She took a bottle out of her bag. It was almost full.

—You have to keep drinking, remember? You told me that.

She drank in short gulps, then I took a long drink. It was half-empty when I finished. I couldn't stop panting. I couldn't catch my breath in the heat. There was nowhere to rest. The only shadows were the dark fringes of the stones scattered across the ground. She crouched down and put her hands over her eyes.

—How did we get here? she said. How did we get *here*?

—Stop it, Mom, just stop it. I'm going.

I turned and started up the hill. *Whatever you think.* That meant it was my call. It was my fault if it went wrong. I walked faster, pushing my hands against my knees as I climbed, calculating the angles to the house. It seemed such an innocent mistake, like losing your car in a parking lot. But it wasn't innocent at all, not here. It was playing with your life. It was spinning the gun and holding it to your head. I retched but nothing came out, not even a taste of acid. I bent over with the dizziness. The heat. The fucking heat. Beating down on you. Pulling you down.

I DRANK THE last of my water, the bottle flashing in the light. Had we turned around somehow? I could see her behind me and the house above me and the blue mountains in the distance, but the rest blurred together in greys and browns.

Just leave me, Ashe, she'll say. Go for help. You have no choice.

It has to be here, I said out loud. It has to. I'll get us out, don't worry. I'll find the river.

She was far behind me, limping the way Sheila limped. Don't stop. Don't fall. I can't . . . I'll try, but I can't. Carry you.

I REACHED A crest in the hill, and below, an outcrop of boulders looked familiar. I ran down the slope, my teeth clacking together. Then I saw the cleft where we'd climbed up, and I walked to the edge of the bank. There was the riverbed below, and up the hill was the house to the left, just as I'd remembered it. Nell was at least a hundred yards behind. I sat on a boulder waiting for her. It was almost six thirty. It would take two solid hours to get back to the car, and we had no flashlight with us. I rested my head on my arms and listened to her feet on the stones.

—Stupid, she said, breathing hard.

I nodded, without looking at her.

—When does it get dark? I said.

—I don't know.

—It took two hours to get here from the car. Do you have any water?

She took the bottle from her bag. It had two inches left.

—That's all we have, I said.

I turned from her and climbed down the bank.

We were walking along the grooves of the clay riverbed with the wind to our back. The orange sun was low in the sky. The shadows fell toward us. We were walking upstream. The river would be flowing directly into us, carrying us back into the desert. There were yellow streaks in my eyes from the sun. They turned black when I looked down, and green and blue when I blinked. They bounced across the ground and sky and blotted out the hands of my watch. I could make it alone if I hurried. I could drive the car and get help. But I couldn't leave her, and she couldn't go any quicker. She was limping badly as it was, her head right down.

The sun was below the top of the mountains. She was dragging her feet, then she fell to her knees on the gravel.

—I'm sorry.

—Just a little farther, I said.

—I can't.

I sat down beside her.

—It doesn't matter. It'll be pitch-black soon.

—I'm sorry, she said.

—It's all right.

—We're stuck here all night. I didn't eat enough. My legs won't move.

—It's okay, I said.

In the trunk of the car there were five bottles of water. I might still be able to make it. I'd pour them down my throat, one after the other. I'd sleep in the car and come back in the morning. But she'd be gone. I knew that. She'd have wandered off and I'd never find her again.

—I thought we'd make it, she said. I thought it was closer.

—Are there snakes here?

—Tuck the ends of your pants in. They won't bite if you don't bother them. Let's sit over there.

I helped her up, and we hobbled over to a boulder in a flat patch of clay and sat with our backs to the rock.

—Ten hours, she said. Maybe less. We've had two bottles each. We'll be okay until the morning. You all right?

—I'm thirsty.

—I'm sorry, she said.

I put my arm around her, and she laid her head on my shoulder. The orange sky over the mountains turned blood-red then grey then, slowly, black. The rocks blurred and vanished and the ground danced around us in the dark.

A CLATTER UP the riverbank. I strained to hear, but the wind blew hard, and it was lost. Shapes undulated over the ground, shapes everywhere, bending and twisting. You'd hear something before you saw it. I listened hard until the sounds drifted. I rested my head on the rock. I kept waking to the gusting wind and the stabbing pain in my throat, looking up at the stars in confusion, the outside seeming to be inside because of the heat and the silence. I listened for stray noises, then I fell back asleep.

—ASHE.

I woke in the pitch-black.

—What?

—You know that empty gas station on Highway 9? Just north of us? Near the old baseball diamond.

—Yeah.

—It has that big roof over the gas pumps. You know the one . . . Her voice trailed off.

I waited and then closed my eyes.

—You can park there if you want to, she said.

The wind lifted, a hot dry current rippling over my arms and face.

—If it was snowing. If it was a storm, you could park there . . .

The wind built up until it was whistling again.

—Say you were scared and your arms tightened up on you . . . you could rest there for a while. Or you could keep going. You could choose to keep going.

I waited, without raising my head.

—Ashe, I just wanted to get home. I didn't want to stay there. I wanted to get out of the snow. I couldn't see the road. He told me to slow down, he kept shouting at me, but I kept going. I told him, I'm not stopping here, we're going straight home, that's *that*.

The wind dropped. I felt her turn toward me. She was staring at me.

—*Ashe?*

I didn't move.

—Ashe?

She touched my forehead.

—What? What is it? I said.

—I woke you. Sorry.

—What?

—No. Nothing, she said. Sorry. I didn't know you were asleep.

—Do you have any water? I said.

—No.

—Where's your bottle?

—I dropped it way back there.

—I thought you had some.

—No, she said.

—Aren't deserts supposed to be cold at night?

—Some are. Just not this one. Not in the summer.

I leaned against her, thinking of the gas station. They put a wire fence around it for a while, but it was pulled down bit by bit. I used to go there with Will. If you held the nozzle to your nose, you could still smell the gasoline in the tank deep underground. There were scrape marks on the floor where the gas station man used to lean back on his chair, waiting for cars. I imagined the two of them parked there. It didn't matter anymore, it was pointless, but it kept coming back to me. A few minutes, that's all it would have taken. A few minutes to calm down. With so many minutes wasted. A desert full of them.

SHE SHOOK ME awake.

—We can walk now, she said.

The moon was bright, almost full, lacking only a sliver.

—Did I sleep long? I said.

—A few hours.

I could see rocks and shrubs and the bank across the riverbed. I tried to stand up, but my legs were numb. I rested against the boulder until the pins and needles died down.

—You have any water? I said.

—No. I told you. It's in the car.

—My tongue's sore.

—Come on. Let's go, she said.

We walked slowly, holding hands, avoiding the rocks.

—*There!* I shouted.

The white roof in the moonlight. We'd been right beside the car the whole time. We hurried over the scrubland and up the hill. You couldn't see the campground in the dark, just the top half of the car poking out from the brush. Nell found the keys and unlocked the trunk. I grabbed a bottle of water and poured it down my throat, letting it flow over my face and chest. It hurt to drink. I felt dizzy and crouched with my hands on the ground.

—You knew about that house, I said.

—I didn't know about it.

—No, don't *bother*. Don't even bother. Just tell me. You knew about it, didn't you?

—Whatever you say, Ashe. If you want me to say I did, then I'll say that.

—You knew.

—If you say so.

She opened the front door, and the roof light blocked out the desert and sky. There was only the car now. I gave up asking her about the house and lay down on the back seat and listened to the engine start, a chuckling roar, then a deep steady rumble. We were driving home, just like that, we were going home without anything having happened. The engine hum pressed me gently to the seat. *Tomorrow*, it said, *and the day after that, and the day after that. Everything ahead, everything that's coming.*

I turned on my side and fell asleep.

23.

W**HEN** I **WOKE**, it was morning and I was lying on the back seat of the car in front of the motel. Flies were hitting my face. I waved them away and reached down for my sunglasses and put them on and then took a long drink of water from a bottle. If I kept perfectly still, the pain in my head stopped beating. Under the windshield wiper was a note:

couldn't wake you—
cabin door unlocked

The words were scratched in blue ink. She'd used the motel's pen. I'd tried it myself. You had to press down and scribble hard to make it work. I'd jabbed the point into the wall to get the ball moving, but that never works. It's never the ball that's stuck. It's always the ink that's dried up in the vein. *Couldn't wake you.* She'd left me here with the windows open, and the cabin door unlocked. In this hovel, with freaks coming and going day and night. But that was her, dancing on a bridge, racing in a storm, wandering in a desert.

I saw Sister Martha sitting on the steps of the office. I dropped

ALAN GIBNEY

my head and ran my fingers through my hair and opened the door
quietly. I got out and quickly walked to the cabin. For some reason,
I glanced back, and there she was waving at me. Leave me *alone*,
woman. I walked over to her. Jesus Christ, just leave me alone.

—I didn't want to miss you, she said. I thought . . . when she
didn't come this morning . . . I thought she might be sleeping in.

—She's still sleeping, I said. (Talking stabbed my eyes.) We
got back late.

—I understand.

—Do you want me to wake her?

—No, no, let her sleep. Maybe you could tell her that I'll be at
the abbey. I'd love to see her.

—I'll tell her.

—Tell her I'll show her the rock garden, she said.

—Okay, I will.

—Any time is fine with me. I'll be back there in an hour. Any
time after that.

—I'll tell her, I said.

She gave me back our umbrella and I walked with her down
the driveway, not knowing how to break off.

—You're burnt, she said. You should stay out of the sun.

My cheeks were still hot. Why were they still hot when anything else would have cooled by now? At the main road, she pressed
a finger to my neck.

—That's a bad burn, she said.

—It feels hot.

—You have to be careful. Don't go out in the sun anymore.

Here. She turned up my collar. Don't get another burn. You'll be in a bad state if you do.

She brushed my hair back.

—Take this. She took a chain with a blue medallion from around her neck and put it over my head. It's been blessed. It's very special. I got it in Italy.

—Thank you.

—I got it because of your sister, in remembrance of her.

—What do you mean?

—It was blessed for her.

—My sister?

—It's sad, I know.

—She won't tell me properly, I said, nodding toward the motel. I think she should tell me everything.

—She didn't explain what happened?

—No. It's not fair. It's my sister and no one will tell me. Everyone's hiding things. She'll never tell me. She just won't.

—That's not right. You need to know about your own flesh and blood. It's a part of you. She shouldn't keep that from you . . . She's not going to talk to me, is she?

—She will. She's sleeping. She'll talk to you.

She shook her head.

—We can go back, if you want, I said. I can wake her.

—No. I don't want to do that. I don't want to force her. It has to be of her own free will.

—I told her about you, I said. I don't know why she didn't meet you.

—She doesn't want to, that's why.

—I don't know. Maybe not.

—No, she said, shaking her head.

—You were there at the time, weren't you? You know what happened. Can't you at least tell me?

—She'll be very angry if I tell you.

—She won't find out. I won't tell her. I just want to know for myself.

She took my hand.

—Come on. Let's get out of the sun.

We walked over to a bus stop with an awning and sat down.

—I do think you have a right to know, she said. Such things shouldn't be kept secret, like they never even happened. There's too many secrets in this world. What has she told you already?

—Just that she was pregnant and she came here and something happened to the baby.

—She was seventeen and unmarried. You know all that, right?

—Yes, I said.

—Sometimes things like that happen. She'd known the father for only a few weeks, then he left without promising her anything. He didn't even know she was pregnant. So she was in a difficult situation, you understand? She had no money or prospects. She had no mother, and she didn't get along with her father. What was she going to do? How could she take care of a baby on her own? So we tried to help her. We found parents for her child, good parents. But when your mother saw the baby, she wouldn't give it up. The moment she held it, she changed her mind. We tried to persuade her. We all did. *I* did. I tried to persuade her as best I could. I thought it was for the best, you see, to give the baby a fair chance in life. I told her how hard it would be for her. How would she cope? You can understand why I would say that?

—Yes, I said.

—But she wouldn't listen. The moment she saw the baby, she wouldn't listen. It was natural, of course, the maternal instinct kicking in. It's the most natural thing of all. She was scared we were going to force her to give it up, you understand. But we'd never have forced her, never. She didn't understand that. She was so young, and she hadn't slept for days, and the baby was losing weight all the time because her milk was upset. I was terrified for the baby. I thought she might leave with her and go back home. I asked the doctor to come over and make sure the baby was all right. She was just a few weeks old, you see. She was too young to travel. It was extremely hot, just like now, the very same month.

—How did the baby die? I said, wanting her to finish.

She arranged her habit, placing the rosary carefully across her knees.

—The priest came with the doctor. It was the same priest who'd found the couple for the adoption. He wanted to persuade Nell to stay a little longer. But Nell saw them from the window in the dark. She saw these two men walking up the path, and she thought they were there to take her baby away, so she locked the door and wouldn't come out. We tried to get her to open the door, but she wouldn't. And that night she took the abbey car and left with the baby. It was this old beat-up Chevy that kept breaking down. We used it to get up and down the hill. She took it and drove across the desert to get to Nevada. It's much quicker across the desert, you see . . .

—What happened?

It's not easy to tell you this . . . It was in the middle of summer. Desert nights are extremely hot in the summer, *extremely* hot. But she didn't know that, just how incredibly hot it would be . . . She was driving in the desert, and she said she saw a car behind her on the road and thought it might be the police, and she turned off onto a dirt road to get away, and somewhere up that road, the car gave out. It must have been more than ninety degrees out there. The baby was already weak, you see. And staying out there in the heat was . . . well . . . it was too much for her. At some point during that night, the baby passed away. That's what happened. Nell couldn't save her baby. She tried to, but she couldn't. I'm sorry.

I nodded, staring at the road.

—But that wasn't the end of it. After the baby died, Nell did something she couldn't explain later. She wrapped up the baby and took it out into the desert . . . She was gone two days and two nights. They found her lying by a dirt road two days later. Just her, with no baby. She couldn't remember where she'd gone, where the baby was. She said she'd walked for hours and hours and buried her somewhere in the sand. The police got involved, of course. There was a big manhunt for the body. They searched twelve square miles but they never found it.

But I knew where it was, as surely as if I'd put it there myself. By a miner's cabin, under a pile of rocks.

—Then they held a coroner's inquest, and we all had to testify. They tried to make a case she'd harmed the baby on purpose, but there was no evidence for that, not a single thing. The jury declared it an accidental death. All I can remember from the whole thing was the coroner asking her, *Why on earth did you go into the desert?* And her saying back to him, *To stay, sir.*

I'd had enough. I stood up.

—*No*, don't leave. I have to tell you something. I wanted to tell Nell herself, but she won't see me, so I'm going to tell you . . . I was the one who talked to the doctor and the priest. I arranged it all. I told them that we needed to change Nell's mind about keeping the baby. Nell was closer to me than anyone. She trusted me. I spoke with the priest and we planned how to persuade her. Do you know what I'm saying?

—I better go back now, I said.

She held on to my wrist.

—Do you *understand*? She was a child herself. I knew that. And I tried to make her give up her own baby. I decided it was for the best, and I tried to make her give it up. I wanted her to give it up.

I nodded, pulling my hand away.

—Look at me.

Her eyes were wet.

—She won't visit me, she said. She won't. I know that. She wouldn't speak to me after it happened. She wouldn't even look at me. The police said I wasn't allowed to talk to her. But I'm telling you, I want to tell you, I *wanted* her to give up her baby. I did. I did things behind her back so she'd give it up. I did those things, and I can't undo them.

I pulled my hand away again, and still she held on.

—I've confessed it many times, but it makes no difference. I can't accept forgiveness. I didn't want her to keep her baby, you see. I couldn't have one, so why should she? That's how I felt. That's the truth. I have to live with it. I can't live with it, but I have to.

—I want to go, I said.

—No, don't go just yet . . . I've told you everything now. Now you know what happened to your sister. I'd never call her your half-sister. I don't believe in that. She was your full sister.

—She *was* my full sister, I said.

—Yes, she was.

—No, I mean she was my real sister, not my half-sister.

—Not your full sister, she said.

—Yes, my full sister. My dad came back. He came back from the war, and he married my mom.

—No, she said, shaking her head.

—Yes, he did. He came back and found her.

—But . . . how could I have known that? she said. My God, I told Nell she'd never see him again. That he'd had his fun. A man like that, getting a young girl pregnant and just walking off.

—He did come back.

—A man like that. That type. Preying on the innocent. I told her to forget about him. You can't rely on such a man. They never come back to you.

—He came back and married her, and he died ten years ago. They were still married.

—No. She held my hand tight. How could I have known that? Ashe. Ashe? Tell me. How could I know he'd come back?

I yanked my hand away and ran up the driveway.

—*Ashe! Ashe! Ashe!*

She kept calling my name. By the time I reached the cabin, she'd stopped. I sat outside on the step breathing hard. Her medallion hung around my neck. I ripped it off and threw it away. For a while, I stared at it on the ground. Then I walked over and scraped the red dirt over it and went inside. Nell was awake, lying on the bed. I sat beside her in her warm milky smell.

—You're burned, I said, touching her face.

—So are you. I had to leave you in the car. I'm sorry. I couldn't wake you up.

—It's okay.

—What's wrong?

—That Sister Martha was here again, I said.

—What? Did you talk to her?

—She cornered me. I had to.

—I told you not to talk to her. What did she say?

—She was looking for you.

—But what did she say? *Tell me.*

—She told me about the baby. She said it died.

—No! That *whore!* she shouted. That *fucking* whore! It's a *lie*, Ashe. Jesus Christ, she's lying to you.

She jumped up, pulled on her shoes, and ran outside.

—Where is she? she said.

I pointed to the road.

—Stay put, she said. I ran beside her along the path to the bus stop. There was no one on the street.

—She was here, I said. Maybe she's in the church.

We ran over to the church, but the doors were locked. There was no one there. Nell sat on the steps.

—That bitch. That *vicious* bitch, she said. She was *horrible* when I was here. She made up stories about me and told them to everyone in town. She snuck into my room at night when I was asleep and got into bed with me. Do you know why? Because she was in love with me. That was her dirty little secret. That's why she was hiding away in the abbey in the first place. She only likes women, you see. Not men. All the nuns knew about it. She told me she wanted to take care of me. She wanted me to run away with her.

—Why would she say the baby died?

—She's mad, that's all. She probably believes it. She's mixed up all these crazy stories in her head. I told the priest about her and they ordered her to go to another abbey, but she wouldn't go.

—She did look crazy.

—Did she? she said, glancing at me.

—Yes. Her eyes were really strange.

—She's dangerous. She should have been locked up long ago.

That one startled look of Nell's and I knew the nun had told the truth. It wasn't a guess. I knew. But that didn't mean Nell was lying to me. It wasn't anything like a lie. It's just some things you keep for yourself. She'd tried to give me a sister in place of Will, but she'd kept one thing for herself, that night in the desert. I could take it away from her if I wanted, but I wasn't going to.

—Let's just go, I said.

She was crying.

—Why did she say that? What gives her the right to tell filthy lies like that?

I put my arm around her.

—It doesn't matter, Mom. I didn't believe her anyway. You told me she was nuts.

I pressed my face into her hair.

—That crazy bitch, she said.

—Come on. Let's go.

We walked back to the cabin. She limped as she walked. She'll be old someday, I thought. We'll walk together like this.

It's up to you now, Ashe, Will would have said. *It's up to you. No one else knows, no one else cares. There's only you.*

BACK IN THE cabin she cried in the same way she cried when my father died. I cried too, agreeing with her. There was nothing to be said about it, nothing to be angry at, nothing to learn. I agree. Her crying showed how cruel it is, how unnecessarily cruel. I agree, I agree. But I also knew she would tire, you can't cry like that forever. Eventually you tire, like a fish on a line. No matter how far it swims, or how often it runs, it tires. As long as the line holds, you can pull it in. It's never enough, the crying said, the life we shared, the secrets we kept, the promises we made. I agree, I agree. I'll never accept it, everything wasted, everything lost. I will never accept it. I agree. The fish slows down, and you know the fight's over, and you respect the fish for fighting, but it's over. There's nothing more to it, we tire, we forget. In the end, she stopped crying.

I SAT IN the front of the car as we drove out of the motel. Lynn from the diner was hanging out on the sidewalk with two teenage boys. The boys were laughing together, but she was standing apart with her arms crossed. I waved and she stepped toward the road with her hands up, smiling. I wanted to take her with us. She could sit with me and we'd talk and laugh the whole way back.

A mile out of town, I asked Nell to stop by the side of the road and I ran over and picked some desert flowers. For Sheila, I said when I got back to the car. Nell took them and wrapped them carefully in a map of California and put them on the back seat.

Driving through the desert, I watched the mirage on the road ahead, the blue-and-brown horizon stretching flat to the edge of my vision. I could imagine Will sitting behind us in the car but not the little girl. God, how I wished I could ask Sister Martha one last question. One question for myself. *What colour were my sister's eyes?* It was the only thing I knew about her, those two different eyes. It was the only thing I could have known about a girl three weeks old. Was it even true? Did she have those eyes at all? I so wanted her to have those eyes—two different eyes for two different babies. I watched the wavering salt beds far down the valley disappear behind the rock cliff bordering the road. We were rising out of the desert into the mountains, leaving behind the dry riverbed where we'd wandered, the river gone and still there, the way Will was gone and still there.

ACKNOWLEDGEMENTS

I WOULD LIKE TO THANK Zindle Segal for his extraordinary humanity and wisdom, Don Thomas for his invaluable guidance and mentorship, and Patrick Crean for his great sensitivity and vision and the brilliant insights he provided as editor. I would also like to thank Chandra Wohleber, Allyson Latta, and Al Zuckerman for their contributions to the novel, and Morty Mint for all his work on my behalf as my agent. Most of all I would like to thank my wife, Eva, my children, Yvonne and Pierce, and my whole family for all the support they gave me each and every day.